GW01451603

His
Christmas Muse

by

J. J. Ranson

The His and Hers Christmas Series

Copyright Notice
This is a work of fiction. Names, characters, places, and incidents are either the product of the author's imagination or are used fictitiously, and any resemblance to actual persons living or dead, business establishments, events, or locales, is entirely coincidental.

His Christmas Muse

COPYRIGHT © 2024 by Julie J. Ranson

All rights reserved. No part of this book may be used or reproduced in any manner whatsoever without written permission of the author or The Wild Rose Press, Inc. except in the case of brief quotations embodied in critical articles or reviews.
Contact Information: info@thewildrosepress.com

Cover Art by *Teddi Black*

The Wild Rose Press, Inc.
PO Box 708
Adams Basin, NY 14410-0708
Visit us at www.thewildrosepress.com

Publishing History
First Edition, 2024
Trade Paperback ISBN 978-1-5092-5839-0
Digital ISBN 978-1-5092-5840-6

The His and Hers Christmas Series
Published in the United States of America

Dedication

To Mom.
You gave me all the encouragement
to pursue my crazy dreams.

**Also by J. J. Ranson
and published by The Wild Rose Press, Inc.**

She Danced Anyway
Elizabeth Alter wants to work and dance in 1920s New York. Will she avoid the trap of marriage and live the independent life she dreams of?

Chapter 1

Sylvie

The little café on Foushee Street was a perfect place to meet a stranger, with its quiet booths nestled among lighted ficus trees. I got there half an hour early for my date with "Tim." His sense of humor came across so vividly on the screen. I wasn't exactly sure what he looked like, as the only photo on his profile was a blur of dark hair and a wide smile, the kind celebrities toss at the camera. He exuded success, a huge selling point.

I caught sight of a head of dark hair and the flash of a red sweater near the door. My heart leaped into my throat, and I hastily gulped some water. Completely out of dating practice, I licked my lips and wished I'd checked my makeup a few minutes earlier.

I stood as he approached, even though I too wore the promised color. I'd gone with a flowy red top and black girlfriend jeans. He placed a hand on the opposite chair. I gasped and nearly choked at the sight of him.

"Timmy?" I 'bout near squeaked his name. This could not be happening! What the heck? My boyfriend from high school?

And still with that boyish smile I remembered so well from when he stood on my doorstep to take me to our senior prom. Behind the chair, he met my gaze, looking confused.

"What?"

"Birmingham City High?"

"Oh, my gosh! Anna. Sylvester. Bradley." He intoned my name with an exaggerated drawl, just like he'd addressed me in high school.

Before I went to college and crafted a nickname, everyone called me Anna Sylvester, very southern. Girls sported double names among the first families of Birmingham and in most of the South.

Timothy Alan Jones hadn't been very social as a high school junior. But I, Anna Sylvester, plucked him out of the football lineup and pulled him into my busy, social world. As a majorette in the marching band, I had swarms of friends who longed only to date a handsome football player. I lived every teen girl's dream in the hot, sunny South where one's family lineage meant everything. Timmy tagged along, seemingly in awe of my family's lifestyle.

We weren't rich. Let me make that clear—painfully clear.

When I was about ten years old and noticing the differences in things my inner circle of friends had—clothes, fancy lunchboxes and their contents—I asked Momma if we were rich.

"Not rich, dah-lin'. Just comf-table," she'd drawled, not lifting her yellow-haired head from her romance novel. A long, drawn-out emphasis on the "comf" was how her deep Alabama accent infected her words. We had been comfortable because of Momma's family. Daddy did his dead-level best to keep us on the edge of broke, or so it seemed to my younger self. I didn't always understand what Momma and Daddy were fighting about, so I read books on my bedroom window seat, waiting for their angry voices to stop.

There are lots of railroad tracks in Birmingham. Though Timmy wasn't from the other side of them, he might as well have been, according to the whispered words I overheard at home. My parents and their annoying focus on social class. Sigh. But even I wasn't prepared for how awkward he acted around my folks and their friends at the country club. His head had swiveled around like a possessed girl in a scary movie, taking in all the high fashion, the smoke-tinged laughter of rich old men, and the sashay of women in hose and heels even on humid summer nights.

I'd watched Timmy out of the corner of my eye, occasionally touching his thigh with my hand to reassure him. I'm not a touchy-feely person at all, but he had brought out a kindness in me. A smattering of empathy, too, I suppose.

Birmingham Acres Country Club hadn't been my scene either, but my parents had a monthly reservation which required the attendance of me and my sister Constance Miller. Her middle name was Daddy's great-grandmother's surname. Mine belonged to my maternal grandmother. Often, we got to bring a friend, which eased the tension that coiled inside my gut like a snake. I had preferred to ignore Momma's embarrassing conversations with her friends.

For two years, Timmy and I were quite an item, until college pulled us apart. I wandered a mere hour southwest to the University of Alabama in Tuscaloosa, enjoying dorm life and all that a huge university offered. Timmy got a football scholarship to play at a private college, Birmingham Southern College. I figured he'd never leave town. I can't remember exactly how we broke up, but I recall thinking once that I didn't want to be stuck in Birmingham my whole life. We didn't move on to other people; we just stopped talking. Isn't that what usually happens when two people have little in common anymore?

Seeing him right in front of me—both of us away from the familiarity of our old lives—made my hand shake as I took a sip of water. I don't know whether I felt excitement or disappointment. I mean, really, I'm starting a new dating life and the first guy out of the gate is an old beau? Silently, I told God I didn't appreciate his sense of humor. So not funny.

Rustling of paper drew me back from the past.

"Well, well, Anna Sylvester, how are you?" Tim put down the menu and folded his hands on top of it.

"People call me Sylvie now. And I'm doing okay. Do tell…what brought you to Richmond?"

Tim leaned back and smiled, his teeth as pearly white as I remembered from high school. His football teammates had teased him back in the day about a future toothpaste modeling career.

"Work, of course. I hated leaving Birmingham, but this place has grown on me. What about—"

"How long have you been here?" I interrupted, wanting to keep the attention on him for a bit longer. How would I describe what was going on in my work life? I'm not sure of it myself sometimes.

"I started working with a sports development group about four years ago. Before that, I was in Birmingham working at B-S."

"B-S?"

"My college, Birmingham Southern. Remember? Played football there. I got in good with the A.D."

I frowned.

"Athletic Director. Sorry, talking shorthand is a bad habit in sports."

A server showed up at my elbow, so I picked up the menu and ordered my favorite salad. Tim chose a grilled chicken sandwich.

He lifted his glass of icy water to his lips, looking over the rim at me. Drops of condensation from the glass splashed on the dark wood table.

"Your turn, Sylvie. Man, that's hard to say. Old habits, you know."

I smiled and nodded while I tucked a strand of hair behind my right ear. Old habits. Timmy was an old habit I didn't think I wanted to take up again. But he sat across from me, and Momma always insisted on politeness.

"Well, um…I've been here for about eighteen months. I work for a strategic consulting firm out of Nashville. Supposed to set up an outpost here." I gestured with air quotes around "outpost."

"Strategic consulting, huh? You always were the smartest girl in school."

And that pretty much sums up our date. Tim kept lobbing compliments about how smart I'd always been, while I tried to get information about his time back in Birmingham and what he'd been up to since his move here.

Tim used a lot of complicated descriptions about sports and its management in Virginia universities. I stifled a yawn when our plates were almost empty.

I went home from that date with the start of a headache, probably cuz I didn't get what I wanted—a date with an exciting new man.

Still, I couldn't call the entire evening a bust. I can swagger all I want about making my way in a new city, but you can't take Alabama out of a girl. The touchback to Birmingham made this homesick girl feel better—less lonely.

Hearing a familiar accent along with enjoying Tim's fun approach to life made me smile when I replayed our date. He promised to reach out again. Half of me wanted to move into the future, and the other half could be happy reverting to the comfortable past. I wasn't sure about picking back up with an old boyfriend.

It's okay to be unsure. Isn't it?

Chapter 2

Sylvie

Tiny white droplets slid down my kitchen window. I hadn't noticed them as I pecked away at my laptop until the ping of sleet made me look up. I'm finally seeing snow, the mysterious white stuff I read about as a kid in Birmingham. Alabamians know nothing of snow, let me tell you.

My fingers flew over the keyboard. I grinned at the screen as I reviewed my potentially witty response to Joey_Runs_With_Scissors on the dating platform I recently joined. I clicked send, then rose from the stool and pushed it under the granite countertop, which currently served as the desk of my home office.

I stared down at the street traffic below. The morning snow would soon keep people home. Friday's labor stalked the hearts and minds of Richmond's workforce, but if the snow kept up, I heard it might thwart their efforts to get into office buildings. Southern towns struggle to manage snowfall, so I've learned from the news anchors.

The glass gave off a chill, and I shivered. Before the pale gray atmosphere deepened my already anxious mood, I speed-dialed my best friend back in Birmingham.

"Sylvie! Why are you calling during work hours on a Friday? What's wrong?"

Angie's bubbly chatter always makes me smile. I loved my talkative friend, so grateful for how Angie—Angela to her mother—fills uncomfortable silences when we're out with others. Small talk and girlish chatter aren't my style anymore. I'm the queen of awkward pauses and saying the wrong thing.

And this runs completely counter to my cheerleading days. My mother and sister were both cheerleaders. As a toddler, I mimicked my sister Constance Miller, waving the stringy pom-poms and kicking my legs. Apparently, I had been coordinated, so Momma decided we were definitely "a cheering family." Eye roll. I always liked sports and physical activity, so I just went along. Pleasing Momma—now there's the one true path of least resistance. Until, of course, I got an interesting gift from Daddy's sister, my Aunt Carol, for my twelfth birthday. It altered my teen years in ways I still feel today.

"Angie, it's snowing here! Can you believe I might see my first white Christmas?"

Not that I really believed that would happen. Weather people were notoriously inaccurate. And Christmas was still a month away.

"That would be almost as surprising as you having a boyfriend during the holidays!" Angie laughed at her own joke, knowing full well she was the only one who could get away with saying such a thing to me.

"News on that front."

"Wait, what? You have a boyfriend? How'd you get that far without me knowing? I cannot believe you'd hold out on me. Uh-uh. wait…a…second. You're joking, right?"

I flopped onto the black leather sofa, tucked my feet

under a fluffy white throw, and settled in to share the whole truth, nothing but the truth, with Angie. The nature of our relationship was facts, facts, and more facts. From me, that is. Like a tormented teen, Angie enjoyed throwing in a lot of feelings when she shared her stories about work, love, and everything else. Feelings from Angie were fine, but my feelings? Uh no, please don't make me talk about them.

"Well, actually, no boyfriend. But I've got two dates planned. And I already had one."

"What! Why am I just hearing about this?"

I brushed my dark blonde bangs out of my eyes and leaned forward off the sofa to check my hair in the beveled mirror that hung over a dove-gray console table. My hair needed a trim, but I'd been too busy lately to think about making a salon appointment and would never get one now, with Christmas so close. I'd just be "Shaggy Sylvie" this winter. Good heavens, Momma would have a kitten if she got a glimpse of my poor grooming.

I wondered if I should grow out my shoulder-length hair, and just trim the bangs myself. I pursed my lips at my reflection. Would Momma notice at Christmas?

"Yoo-hoo! Anna Sylvester?"

I imagined her staring at her phone like our call cut off. I hesitated to tell her about Timmy. Um, Tim, as he now calls himself. She had such romantic dreams about me and Tim back in high school. She'd lived vicariously through whatever boy angst I experienced with him. Both of us had mostly crushed on boys, getting little attention in return.

Angie had been a little pudgy, but so pretty, with her dark curls, enormous brown eyes, and perfect skin. Not much dating action, though, until we got out of high school. She really blossomed in college. Working at her family's shop and commuting to college created enough stress, Angie lost the fifteen pounds she'd despaired over for years. She cut her hair into a gorgeous, layered bob and became the toast of campus. I couldn't keep up with her dating escapades during her senior year.

She'd majored in business at Birmingham-Southern, where Tim played football. Our freshman year, she updated me on his activities, but I lost interest in the gossip…and Timmy. An unrequited crush on another business major had diverted all my attention from the value of an old, familiar beau.

"I'm still here. Well, you see…I met a guy last night for dinner. He'd rescheduled once, so I didn't want to jinx it."

"Oh, this sounds good. I'm all ears. From the online dating site, yes?"

"Yes, all three."

"Who is this new Sylvie?" Her high-pitched voice tinged with amusement.

"Do you wanna hear about last night's date?"

"Uh, yeah…spill it, girlfriend."

"Remember Timmy? From high school?"

"Of course, I do, but what—"

"He was my date last night."

Angie huffed on the other end of the line.

"He's in Richmond?"

"Apparently."

"So, that's strange. So how did it go? Is he still gorgeous?" Angie giggled like her sixteen-year-old former self.

"At first, my brain was yelling no, no, no. I mean,

Ang, no dates since I've been here, and Timmy shows up? What kind of sick joke is that? The universe is against me."

"For real."

"Thanks for your support, my friend."

"Oh, hey, I didn't mean anything by it. Just agreein' with ya. Gimme details. How did the date end? Did he ask to go out again?"

"I suppose he did…"

In my head, I replayed last night when we left the restaurant, and he walked me to my car. The vapor lights on the street had just started to flicker on as darkness settled in. Tim looked kind of happy to be around someone familiar. He'd said he didn't have much of a social life, even though he'd been on Flirtable since the summer. Had I done anything to encourage him? I hope not.

New city. New life. New man. Right?

"You suppose?"

"He mentioned getting back in touch with me. On the site, anyway. I did not offer my phone number."

"Yikes. What're you gonna do?"

"Go on two dates this weekend. Fingers crossed."

I closed my eyes and took a deep, hopeful breath. Something had to click in my personal life. I'd been alone too long here, away from family, and always missing my dearest friend.

"I miss you, girlie," tears making my voice shake.

"Oh man, I sure wish I could be there with you this weekend! This will be magnificent."

I held up my hand like she was there in the room.

"Hold on there, little lady," I deepened my voice and southern accent, so I sounded like my dad. "Just first dates, that's all. Probably will be a bust. Let's just wait and see." I chewed on the skin at the edge of my thumbnail, where it felt rough.

"I don't believe it. We're only thirty-two. Being an old maid is not in your future, or mine."

I shook my head and gazed at my outstretched hand. The nails were different lengths, and what was up with my cuticles? Good grief, all work and no play had wrecked my grooming habits.

"I wish I had time for a manicure. My hands are atrocious, like I've been scrubbing floors or something. I'm a real Cinderella here. Ha-ha. If Momma could see me in this terrible condition, she'd fuss a blue streak."

"Hang on."

From across the miles, Angie whispered to herself as she typed on her phone. "Okay. Here's a place near you. They take walk-ins. Call them."

My phone dinged as her text message arrived. She'd sent me a screenshot of a nail shop a couple of blocks away.

"Thanks, Ang. You're the perfect personal assistant. How should I pay you?"

"Aw, gee, that's what friends are for. What're you going to wear on these dates? Are you going shopping? Want me to come along, you know, virtually? I have opinions."

"Don't I know it."

Stretching at my waist from right to left, I watched the snow and sleet hitting the floor-to-ceiling glass window across from me. I hadn't thought much about what I would wear, other than my top color—each date had agreed to wear red so we could pick each other out of a crowd. I couldn't imagine wandering up to each table with a single man, asking, "Joe?" How embarrassing.

"You've gotten quiet. You won't back out on these guys, will you? Simple meetings, right? Last night was a fluke. It's all good from here on out."

"Right, right." I nodded while I went to the window to peer down at the traffic. I counted only a few cars, so perhaps people were hunkering down as the snow accumulated on the roads. Wide black tire tracks were bordered with glistening white snow. I might get my nails done, but only if I walked to the shop. I really didn't want today to be my first day of driving in the snow, not with so much ahead over the next few days.

"Sylvie? You still there?"

"Oh gosh, yes. Sorry. I was looking at the traffic and thinking about my nails. You'll be happy to know I'm considering your advice!"

"For a change. L-O-L!" I swear she slapped her leg. She really is a hoot.

After Angie filled me in on the Birmingham gossip, we ended the call, and I got back to work. I plowed through a long list of emails and polished up two reports started by others on my team. I struggle with perfectionism. Well, that's not entirely true. It's hardly a struggle, considering I excel at being picky. I embrace perfection as often as humanly possible. I reviewed and heavily edited the reports before I sent them up the corporate food chain. My boss expects nothing less.

This will be my second Christmas in Richmond, Virginia. I came here July of last year to establish a mid-Atlantic office for the Nashville-based strategic planning firm I work for. Gosh, the heat sweltered when I moved up here. Not that Birmingham or Nashville are known for refreshing summer breezes, but that middle weekend of July had felt like someone cranked up the sauna. Even my usually cool-as-a-cucumber mother had damp spots on her blouse.

I mostly do marketing consulting. I also manage a twenty-two-year-old straight out of a local university who is trying to break into the field. *Manage* is a weird term for our relationship. We meet virtually, and she's attended only one online meeting with me and my boss. Mindy is a nice kid. Smart, too. She keeps me on my toes. I only wish she could write worth a crap. Not having to edit her work sure would save me a ton of time.

Business had been almost-booming in my little startup office the past year, after a draining and dull initial six months. Between rescheduled meetings with potential clients and then that first Christmas holiday, I feared getting fired. Getting traction had been impossible. I hadn't delivered a single client contract to Patrick, my boss. He was the one who pushed for patience, to my immense surprise. He was usually so hard-charging and greedy for results. Most days, I wanted to cry when nothing happened, or a scheduled meeting fell through at the last minute.

"Things will shake loose, just you wait and see," he'd said so often over the phone.

Doubting that Patrick's patience would remain steadfast into a second year, I began staying up late into the night, searching for potential clients on the Internet. I had to play the odds with the numbers, I erroneously believed. What I needed to do was build relationships—which I'd learned in grad school at Vanderbilt. Still, earning an MBA seemed like wasted years when I couldn't get a prospective client to return my calls.

Cold calls. Gosh, I hate making them. That's all I did at first. I'm pretty outgoing, but connecting to someone brand new, well, it challenges me. It's probably easy breezy for a few people, but I will never be a member of that special clan.

Instead, alone in my apartment-office, I practiced in front of a mirror, introducing myself while I smiled and held out a hand for the required handshake. I kinda got good at it. Patting myself on the back is also part of my office schtick—there's no one else around to squeal, "Good job, Sylvie!"

The second week of January this year, my ringing phone jolted me out of a document review at ten in the morning. It had to be Patrick calling to pull the plug on this disappointing dud of a project. My family tries not to call during the workday.

"Hello?" I answered, stomach twisting itself into a knot.

"Yes, hi, I'd like to speak to Ms. Bradley."

"Oh! Hello."

I hit my head with my knuckles, knowing I should have answered with an appropriate businesslike greeting such as, "Mossmont Consulting." I was so used to six months of unreturned business calls, I'd forgotten how to answer one.

"Ms. Bradley? This is John Jamerson over at Asurian. Returning your call. Sorry we didn't connect in December. Holidays, you know."

"Thank you for calling me back, Mr. Jamerson."

"John. Listen, I read your company's profile. We may need your help. When can we meet? Um…" The sound of rustling papers filled his silence. "Hang on, I'm trying to find my day planner."

"I have some time this Thursday morning. Or early next week?" I offered, fingers crossed that he picked Thursday so I could file a positive report on Friday.

"Do you mind coming to my office, Sylvie? Thursday at ten?"

"Absolutely. Do you have specific questions or projects in mind so I can come prepared?"

"Nah, let's just chat. See where things lead."

"Okay, I'll be there the day after tomorrow. Thank you."

I clicked off the phone and fist-pumped the air. My second appointment in months of churning the soil here. Mossmont's seeds might take to the Virginia clay and finally bloom.

That call inspired me to plow through my contact list again and do some second and third calls to companies who needed our help. Isn't that how John Jamerson put it?

Yes!

As the new year rolled on, the frozen business ground began to soften enough that several times a month I had a presentation to prepare for or a prospect to meet. Back in Nashville, Patrick was so buoyed by the success he started talking about finding office space. I had grown attached to working at the cool white-and-gray granite counter in my kitchen, so I put him off with a promise of "later."

I threw myself back onto the sofa and adjusted the blanket. My naked toes still tingled from the chill they'd caught by the window. The coolness made me wish for carpet instead of the polished cement that was so popular in these downtown lofts. Should I put a fur rug in front of the living room window? I chuckled at the image of a

bear rug in my apartment.
    No way.

Chapter 3

Sylvie

Saturday morning brought more snow flurries, but this time no flakes committed to the cold, black pavement. I was torn between wanting a thick, delicious frosting of snow and wanting to go on two more dates this weekend. Even after the other night's strangeness, social success remained my goal. It was like riding a bicycle. Who knew?

I'd second-guessed myself about setting up the Flirtable.com account. Those doubts flared again when I saw my high school boyfriend across the table. Yet I got through the evening. Maybe I was meant to see a familiar face as I ventured toward the promise of romance. I merely had to figure out a way to keep Tim at arm's length until he got the message. I wasn't sure how to handle him.

Working from home meant I didn't feel constrained by a Monday-through-Friday schedule. Too often, I spent Saturdays on my laptop at the kitchen counter. It wasn't really work if I was sipping Chardonnay. But this was a special day, so I cut the work short for my date preparations. After a few emails, I had the undeniable, very unusual desire to shop.

I love the color red—you know, like the Crimson Tide? But wearing a college sweatshirt would not give me the air of sophistication I needed to impress a new man. And I decided the blouse I wore last night was not right for today's date.

At the mall, I was overwhelmed. So much red! What had I expected, with it being Christmas and all? I needed help.

"Hey, I have a fashion emergency."

I added the perfect begging tone to get her attention. She knows I'm not the pleading type.

"Okay, what's the prob?" I imagined my dear friend pulling her hair up with one hand while eyeing herself in the mirror.

"I need something red. Everything is red!"

"Blouse, dress, pants?"

"Just a blouse or nice sweater. I'm wearing black pants and heels tonight."

"So, this is date two, right? Exciting!"

"Focus, Angie. Tick-Tock. I still need to get back home and pretty up. And shower."

"Anything red with a little print on it? I get that red's the color for your guy to recognize you, but a print will work too, right?"

"Oh yeah, I hadn't considered that. I wore a solid red top on Thursday night."

"Show me somethin'."

I sauntered through the racks, pushing hangers back to get a better look at items. Angie started singing the famous TV time countdown theme. Cute.

I held up a long-sleeved blouse with a bow tied at the neck. "Don't know if you can see it has a black diamond print all over."

"Old lady."

"Oooh-kay." I hung it back on the rack, straightening it with the rest of its mates.

"You're arranging the racks, aren't you?"

"Just being a good citizen, my friend."

"What store are you in?"

"Department store. And before you jump on my store choice, I came to the mall for a broad selection. I'd rather shop at the boutiques downtown, but I'm in a time crunch."

"Well, you're right. They're bound to have something. You can't be in Juniors. Why don't you go over there?"

It wasn't actually a question, but an order from the fashionista. But I'd called for help, so I had to obey.

"All right. But I'm not wearing some skimpy juvenile thing."

Angie blew out her breath.

"While you're walking there, did you think any more about the other night? You never really said if you'd had a good time with Timmy."

"Yes, surprisingly I did."

"Surprisingly? What does that mean?"

I shrugged as I stepped on the beige-and-burgundy carpet holding the tarty-girl department. I quickly scanned the racks. "This doesn't feel promising."

"What? Wait, I'm confused."

"Welcome to my world! No, not him. This department. Hang on." I held up a V-neck blouse with three-quarter-length sleeves. "I love the white polka dots."

"You're a polka dot lovin' girl, that I know. Go try it on, Sylvie. I got time."

I headed to the dressing room.

"How does Timmy look these days? And what's he doing? I was sure he'd stay in the B'ham forever." Angie and I nicknamed our city "the B'ham" because it was shorter to say, and we have always been silly like that.

I started buttoning up the blouse. "He looks good. His hair was quite short, so no cute wavy bangs hanging over his brown puppy-dog eyes like the old days. And he's working for a sports marketing company."

"Hm." Angie was obviously pondering the angles related to my old boyfriend.

"How's this?" I threw my arms wide and posed.

"Love. Love."

"Phew. And I'm supposed to wear red for date three too. Gee. What was I thinking?"

"Clearly, you're out of practice. News flash!" Angie squealed with laughter. Such a good friend. I shook my head.

"I'll just handwash what I wore last night. Or I can go back and get that other blouse. Ha-ha."

"Don't you dare, Anna Sylvester."

Angie may have sounded like her at that moment, but she didn't want me to look like Momma. I could appreciate that.

"Okay, okay."

"Have a great time tonight and tomorrow. When're you calling in your full report?"

"Can you chat tomorrow after I get home? Shouldn't be too late since tomorrow is a coffee date."

"Girl, I will hug my phone till you call. Hey, but if he's amazing, you can call me as late as you want."

"Hilarious. I'm glad I have you in my corner, girl."

"What're friends for? Angie and Sylvie for-ev-ah!"

"Okay, wish me luck. Peace out."

"Luck!" Angie yelled.

I went back to the women's department to look at

that blouse again. It could be a good backup. Even useful for my Christmas trip home to see the family. A petite gray-haired lady whipped her head around in surprise when I shook my head and said, "You're right, Ang. No way."

I continued to browse the tops for something else to add to my dating repertoire. A slinky mesh-like sweater caught my attention, so I considered what I could pair it with from my closet. I folded it over my arm and headed for the cash register.

After paying for the two tops, I made a beeline for the parking lot and headed home.

With three hours to get ready, I poured a glass of Cabernet Sauvignon and scrolled through the Flirtable profiles. Didn't see anybody new and interesting. I scrolled through the messages from Jeff to remind myself about the important details of his life.

****

That date…oh my! The guy made me want to run straight into Tim's arms. Jeff was obviously a nice guy, but he didn't know how to talk to a girl. He kept jumping between topics, barely letting me get a word in. When the bartender slid over the check, I grabbed it and slipped my credit card onto the receipt tray. Jeff's mouth dropped open as he looked between the receipt and my determined expression.

He picked at his beer bottle label till the server returned with my card. Then, I let him walk me to the corner a little way from my car.

"Thank you for giving me a nod on Flirtable, Jeff. I enjoyed meeting you."

We shook hands and stood there, staring at each other until I broke my gaze and turned away.

"Bye, Sylvie. I'll message you."

Please don't, I thought. Walking to my car, I didn't even look back to acknowledge he'd spoken. Would he read all the signals? Poor fella, he needed a big sister to help him out.

Angie would have a fit, literally, when she learned about Jeff. She's never had much patience with men and their "foolishness," as she calls it. If I cared enough, I'd go back and look at his profile and messages—the signs were surely there, and I missed them. Probably not fair to blame myself for things going wrong, but I can't help myself. It's just built in to want to fix things…and people.

I yawned around ten and closed my laptop. Heading to my bedroom, I wondered again whether I should reconnect with Tim after all these years. What about that old high school history? Gosh, we'd been so immature.

That dinner hadn't been a complete disaster, not after the initial shock of a flash from the past. We had laughed about our high school antics. What were the odds that we'd end up in the same city fifteen years after graduation? Maybe I should see him again. He checked all my boxes: good job, right address, still good-looking, and physically fit.

Snuggled under a blanket, I replayed my date with Tim and the text messages I'd received in the past two days. His messages were friendly and personal. The flirty ones had made me blush. I'd giggled as if a boy in high school had given me a seductive wink.

While I was out with Jeff, Tim texted about meeting for coffee the next week. I'd sleep on it before responding. Shouldn't I make him wait, offer some mystery? Are those juvenile antics? When it came to dating, I did not know what I was doing. Yet, with him, I wanted to do things right. We had a history, and he deserved honesty.

Tim had been right for me once. Could he be right for me again? Tim was like slipping into a comfortable slipper. Since seeing him again, I'd thought how easy it might be to go back in time. Did I want easy, or did I want to have some fun trying to figure out what kind of man I wanted for a long-term relationship?

Chapter 4

Pete

So, I was sitting in the Morris Street Cafe yesterday morning when this woman walked past me and dropped her purse on the bench at the next table. She was beautiful. She didn't fit in. Morris's is a real dive of a place, but it has fantastic food, the best coffee, cool staff. It's also nothing to look at. The leatherette on the booths is torn in places, and the wood tables are scratched and pock-marked. Like many places in Richmond, parking is a nightmare, but since it was Sunday, the street offered lots of spaces.

I go there a lot to clear my head. And fill my belly when I don't feel like cooking.

Back to that beautiful lady. I'd never seen her there. She sat across from me, one table over. I had my back to the door to help me focus on my writing notes, which wasn't going well. She positioned herself facing the door. There she was—facing me like we were together, but with two distressed tables between us. Looking back, everything was all wrong. She should have been at my table. I just didn't know it yesterday.

She sat for a long while, nursing a cup of coffee and fiddling with the napkin and silverware. After a while, she started looking at her phone. Frowning at it, to be precise. I do like to be precise when I tell a story.

Eventually, she punched the phone screen with a

slender finger and turned her body to face the wall. I strained to listen. She became agitated, and her whispers became audible. A silky southern accent textured her side of the conversation. Bright pink spots appeared on her cheeks. She gestured wildly with one hand. And then I put it all together.

She'd been stood up by a blind date. I won't go into all the details. I overheard plenty. More than a regular eavesdropper would have tried to hear. Apparently, she'd ventured into the online dating world. Why, I do not know. A woman like her…

She looked about to cry. I hate being around crying women. Don't all guys? My ex was not one to cry. One of the good things I remember about her.

I needed to leave and give this beauty some space. But not before I connected with her. I stopped at her table on my way out.

"What's wrong with men? You shouldn't have to go online to find someone." I tapped a finger on the wood.

She looked up at me, flipping her smartphone facedown onto the table. The bright pink spots returned when her gray eyes met mine. She didn't even try to speak, even though her rosy lips parted slightly. I probably surprised her out of her despair.

I walked out the door, not giving her a chance to respond. She needed to think about that. And I needed to think about what I'd just done. Geez Louise…You call that a connection, Pete?

"Am I the world's biggest idiot?" I stopped beside my car door and shook my head. A guy dressed in black denim from head to toe gave me a sloppy grin. Of course you are, his grin noted…talking to your car?

I shook my head as I slid into the seat. Glancing at

my watch, I realized I would be late picking up my mom for church. I braced myself for her gentle scowl.

****

My phone dinged with a text message. I didn't need the distraction, so I ignored it. The incessant noise continued, telling me my buddies were pestering about the football game. I don't like missing time with the guys over a beer and talking smack about each other's teams, but that draft wouldn't write itself.

As husbands and fathers, all my buddies understand a missed game now and then. There have been years, however, when I've lost an entire season of football or basketball. I have no favorite baseball team, so I go along to get along in the summer. Sports rivalries give guys a reason to gather…and drink beer.

I looked out the window, pondering the next scene. A red car flashed by, and I thought about the cafe girl again. That's my nickname for her. I had to name her because she'd filled my head for hours.

I was in my groove again. Truly a Christmas miracle! The cafe girl was my Christmas muse. She'd even become the model for my detective's work partner, even the parted rosy lips had made the page. I needed to hear that accent again. But not only the accent, I wanted to experience her voice again. A voice wrapped in a deep but feminine richness that's hard to describe, and I certainly couldn't conjure up what exactly she said. I saw her clearly, though. Her quiet loveliness—shiny hair, gray eyes, and translucent skin—enthralled me. My memory of her was a quiet video playing before me.

I bumped my fist against the dining room table and stared at my computer screen. I hated the table. I hated the room. And the whole place. I wanted to go back to my house.

"I need to eat," I said to no one. I hadn't eaten since the morning's toast and coffee.

And I couldn't return to Morris Street Café. They were closed.

I scratched the top of my head, thinking how I could find my cafe girl.

Hmm. Wasn't I the possessive one?

My fingers flew across the keyboard. I would eat when inspiration fled. I prayed she'd stay on my shoulder a bit longer until all my writing needs were met.

****

"All right, John, I hear you."

"I hope you do, Pete. The publisher's breathing down my neck—"

"And you're breathing down mine!" I rubbed my hand down my face. The beard on my chin was rough. I stayed up late writing last night. John's call woke me at eight.

The coffeepot clinked against my favorite Christmas mug as I poured more life into my morning. Santa was pointing his finger at me.

"Okay, okay." John's sigh whispered across the distance between New York City and Richmond.

"John, I appreciate the space you've given me the past month. It hasn't gone well. Until yesterday."

"Did you get your word count over the halfway mark?" John's tone dripped with sarcasm.

"Hey...I thought you were my friend, man." My throat tightened painfully.

"And your agent."

I left the silence alone as I walked to the kitchen window. Rain pattered on the holly leaves; the red berries glistened. If that were snow, they'd be perfect for a Christmas card. But the temperature had risen, and the flurries were gone.

The berries reminded me of her top. She'd kept looking down and adjusting it, like maybe it didn't fit right.

I sighed audibly.

"Pete, you said you wrote last night?"

"Yeah, I wrote all afternoon and night, actually. Got on a roll."

"That's fantastic!" My agent's encouraging tone replaced the sarcastic one. He was like a pouty toddler who'd just been handed a lollipop. Such was the nature of our business relationship. It's all good until I don't satisfy.

"I hate to make promises, but if this writing trend continues, I may hit fifty thousand words in the next week."

"Good. Good."

"I know I'll still be behind, but I'm gaining ground. Gimme till the new year to write 'the end' but promise you won't relay that to Carol. She'll treat it like gospel."

"Nope. I'll say nothing. But I have to tell her you're working on catching up. Okay?"

"Sure, sure. I've been ignoring her emails."

"Hence this call, my man. And…don't forget P.J.'s adoring fans."

I squeezed the bridge of my nose between my thumb and forefinger. Aspirin, where are you?

"Got it. Must run, John. I'll email you mid-week with an update. Promise."

"You better."

Like a resentful teen, I rolled my eyes.

Chapter 5

Sylvie
I came 'round the dog cage fast, almost kneeing a guy in the back. Squatted down, he made quiet conversation with Riley, the Dachshund we've had for a month. Riley's super cute with the richest tan coat I'd ever seen on his breed.

"Hey." The man stands and I have to look up. He's over six feet tall. Handsome, too. Wait…Oh no way. It's the guy from the cafe, the rude one in the dark brown leather jacket.

"Uh, hi." I looked around for Victoria to help him. I had to get away.

"You're…I mean, I saw you—"

"Right." I stepped away. Getting Victoria's attention was impossible when she's showing a dog. She's right, of course. The animals are the focus. I just wished she'd look my way.

Victoria managed the entire pet rescue facility. She also led us on regular Sunday adoption outings in front of a chain pet store. Our goal was to get applications and rehome the animals within a week or two. The adoption process requires human references, so no one gets to leave with a dog at an event.

"I'm sorry. Let me introduce myself. Pete." He thrust a hand at me.

I looked down at it like he had leprosy.

"Sylvie." I squatted down to check Riley's collar, avoiding his handshake. I never expected to see the man from the cafe again. Hoped I wouldn't, that is. What a jerk, telling me how to run my dating life. I didn't sleep well for two nights because of him. When I told Angie about it, she cackled. She found a compliment in what he said.

Out of the corner of my eye, I glanced at his jeans and boots. The boots were brown leather, no scuffs. Like he just polished them. Geesh. I rolled my eyes.

"So, uh…" His voice was low, like he didn't want anyone to know he was talking to me. Just too weird.

"Let me get Danny to help you." I pushed my hands on my thighs and stood. I walked away, happy to put distance between me and…Pete. I shook my head.

Looping around his beat-up green pickup, I saw no sign of Danny. The tailgate was down, and dog hair swirled in the molded metal channels. Where was Danny?

I looked over the truck bed and saw Pete standing by Riley, hands tucked in his pockets. The air was cold, but the sun offered a charming Christmas kind of warmth. Christmas was still weeks away, but I loved the time leading up to the season.

And I guess that's why I walked over to him. Sylvie's holiday spirit!

"So, Pete is it?"

"Yeah." He blinked at me, trying to adjust to my new attitude. Possibly.

"Riley, here, is a Dachshund."

"He's a really nice dog. I think my mom would love him."

"She's a dog person, huh?"

"Ummm, yeah, I think so. We had a dog when I was a kid. Barkley."

"What kind of dog was Barkley?" I asked him, watching him for any sign of dishonesty. My radar was on high alert to this guy.

He looked at me funny and I realized I was squinting at him. I relaxed my face into the polite countenance my momma would prefer I wear at all times.

"Hmm, what was that old mutt? Ha! I guess he was just a mutt. But he was much bigger than Riley here. Are there major differences between big and small dogs?"

"The important differences are between breeds, mostly. Small and large dogs have their own mentalities, but breed characteristics are most important." I smiled when I gazed down at Riley. I wished I could have him in my apartment, but my lease prevented it.

"Do you know about this breed? What is he, anyway?" Pete crouched down again and pet Riley in a gentle, loving way.

"Dachshund." I'd already told him that. What's with this guy?

Pete laughed. "The sausage dog, of course!"

"Dachshunds are curious and affectionate. But the dog's owner must understand his need for a pack leader. If the owner isn't the leader, the dog can take over the house. Humans should always be the boss of any dog."

"He's so small. How could he lead a house?"

I crouched down beside Pete and Riley. I was close enough to see a few fine lines around Pete's dark eyes. I guessed he was older than me by about ten years. Why that mattered was anyone's guess. I didn't plan to date the man. "His size is very relevant. Small dogs often get treated like babies by their owners. Big mistake."

"Okay. Okay. Your opinions are well taken."

"Not opinions. Experience."

"Gotcha." Pete stood and offered a hand to help me up. I grumbled inside and reluctantly took it. I murmured a thank you while my heart strangely beat faster.

I introduced Victoria to Pete, and she immediately started reviewing the paperwork with him. At four in the afternoon, we had precious little daylight left to return the dogs to the kennel.

Danny, the missing man, materialized and asked me to help him load the dog crates into his truck. Other volunteers appeared, and soon the animals were ready to return to the facility.

While Pete was chatting with Victoria, Danny got in his truck. We all had to go back to the building before our work was done. We headed to our vehicles, and I waved at Victoria, hoping she'd cut off Pete's chatter.

Danny's truck whined and whined. No stutter of sound suggested the engine would turn over. I walked over to the driver's side door.

"Hey. What's up?"

Danny hit the worn black steering wheel. "Dang truck. I'm sure it's the alternator. Gonna have to leave it here tonight."

"But the dogs…"

I turned to find Victoria and Pete headed over. Pete was gesturing and talking.

"I have my truck over there. Can I help?"

"Thank you so much, Mr. Monroe!" Victoria offered him the brightest smile.

Pete Monroe. Such a normal-sounding name for a crazed stalker. That's my nickname for him. I mean, he showed up a week later where I was volunteering.

Hello!! Was I the only one to catch on?

Long story short, Pete had an awesome red pickup. The black bed liner wasn't the least bit scratched after we got all the dogs out back at the kennel. We'd been super careful loading the crates, apologizing to him when we banged stuff around the bed. He didn't seem bothered one way or another.

Then, I wanted to smack Victoria. I'm not violent, nor do I cuss. But she made me crazy mad.

What did she do, you ask?

She invited Mr. Monroe to have dinner with our group!

As I drove to the Chinese restaurant Danny had picked out, I considered just going home. But I was cold and starved, and ready for some cashew chicken.

The place was busy like Christmas Eve, and they had no table for six.

"I'll eat with the other volunteers, Sylvie. You and our new pet parent can sit together. Okay?"

It was not okay. Darn it.

Victoria wiggled a finger for me to follow her to the ladies' room. We're in high school now? Yes, I was irritable.

"Listen." She circled around to face me the minute the door closed. "He was asking about you. Maybe he likes you!" Her big brown eyes looked at me with such hopefulness.

I slipped into a bathroom stall, and she did too.

"I don't think that's it. Never mind. It's only for an hour. What harm can come?"

"Harm?"

"Just me thinking out loud. Ignore me."

Our toilets flushed in harmony, and we washed our

hands in silence. My friend watched me in the mirror, so I kept my expression blank. My throat was so tight, I didn't trust myself to speak.

I followed Victoria like her shadow, peering over her shoulder to check what my table mate was doing. His back was to me. She veered to her table, and I headed straight—down the gangplank.

As I approached him, his thick, dark hair sparkled with a few silvery hairs. Hmmm.

Chapter 6

Pete

My dining partner eased into the chair across from me. Her posture was stiff, like she thought I'd bite. I'd already perused the menu and was about to offer to order for us both, but...

"I was dying for some cashew chicken on the way over." She slipped the napkin onto her lap. Then she scanned the menu.

"What if we shared two dishes? Would you like to try something new?"

Cafe girl peered at me over the menu. Her gray eyes conveyed curiosity. Why did I keep getting this feeling I was stepping in it?

"I've eaten Chinese food since I was a kid. I've tried lots of things." She snapped her menu closed and pulled her cellphone out of a black leather purse. The bag was not the huge kind so many women her age carry. What am I talking about? I've no idea how old she is, but she is definitely younger than me.

Anyway, these enormous bags women carry, what's with those? Who needs to lug around a suitcase every day? How much stuff do they need? Even my mom, who's only fifty-nine, has no explanation for those oversized things.

Cafe girl's bag...hold that. *Sylvie*'s bag was smooth black leather, flat bottom. A designer's name on it.

I'm not sure I'd have recognized my cafe girl today without makeup and her dark blonde hair pulled back in a low ponytail. The red of her sweatshirt had made me take a second look in front of the pet store.

She almost knocked me over, literally. My heart started racing the moment I recognized her.

Sylvie, on the other hand, wanted to race away. Or so it felt like to me.

I had to figure out a way to keep her in my orbit. Or me in hers. That sounds weird. Stalker-ish?

While I kept a deadly writing pace through Thursday this past week, my inspiration eventually waned. After two sleepless nights, I decided I'd never see her again. I'd been plotting how to get my story written without a muse, and my scheming had yielded only a few new words on the page.

Then she almost walked into me. The Man Upstairs was shining upon me. What can I say?

Actually, I needed to say something. To her. She'd taken photos of the menu, and I was pretty sure she snuck a snap of me. Interesting.

"Did you go to Bama?" Pointing at the text on her sweatshirt. Yeah, I pointed at her chest.

"Bama, huh? You know the local nickname. Most outsiders talk about the Crimson Tide." She pulled at the hem of the sweatshirt and shifted in her chair.

"One of my buddies went to Alabama. I think he graduated like twenty years ago."

Sylvie dipped her head and pushed loose strands of hair behind her right ear. She did that a lot at the cafe last week too. "Ohhh. Well, I wouldn't know him." Then she laughed, a throaty sound I hoped to hear again.

"Why did you take photos of the menu? Just

curious."

"Sending to my friend Angie. She still lives in Birmingham."

"It's okay, but…did you take one of me, too?"

"Of course! I sent that to Angie, too." She laughed again—music to my ears.

I waved that off and shook out my napkin and put it on my lap.

Her wariness didn't surprise me when we got to the restaurant. She obviously hadn't wanted to take this table with me. I'm not blind and can recognize when a woman's eyes dart around in desperate hope of escape.

Getting her talking about herself had relaxed the atmosphere, and she didn't seem in flight mode anymore.

Finally, the server approached our table. The other group, seated two tables away from us, already had glasses of water and beers.

I waited while she ordered her cashew chicken. The server patiently answered my question about the sweet and sour pork, and I told him what I wanted. Neither of us ordered beer.

"Sylvie," I spoke her name like it was a butterfly's wing, soft and fragile. She watched me, and I detected a return of wariness. She didn't trust me, and I wasn't sure how to win over my muse. I really needed to get her on my side.

"I think perhaps we got off on the wrong foot."

She snorted a laugh and covered her mouth.

"Really?" Her velvety accent didn't match the sarcastic tone. "Angie thinks your comment about me and online dating was a compliment. It was kind of hurtful, you know?"

"Well, I can—"

"Stop. A strange man taps my table and comments on my love life. And walks off like he's God or something." Her face twisted. Was it disbelief or disgust? I needed to figure out which.

My muse shouldn't be disgusted by me, right? I didn't think it worked that way. I've never had a muse, but I sure needed this one to cooperate for the time being.

"Yeah. I'm very sorry about that. In my defense, I was having an awful day. Work stuff." I tried to pose myself in the most sympathetic way.

She scoffed and stared me down. But while she considered me, I detected a glimmer of interest, or even forgiveness. My apology was clearly heartfelt. I put on an earnest expression, but she remained silent.

I held up my hands in surrender.

"Okay. Okay. I get it. I pulled a Neanderthal move. Completely unfair to you. And…I admit, a stranger shouldn't speak like that to someone. I was raised better. My mother would love to tell you about my raising, I'm sure."

"Huh." Sylvie unwrapped her silverware while she listened to me. Her gaze was still wary, but she was softening. I was sure of it.

From very wary in the parking lot to slightly wary at the restaurant, Sylvie then began to lean in. Just a little, perhaps a negligible amount, so little I couldn't be sure I'd get this turned around. I wasn't confident this would play out well for me.

"What's your story, Sylvie?" I had to know her. Understand her essence. Gotta keep the vision and sound of her in my head for the next few weeks while I cranked out those words.

"What do you want to know?"

Our food showed up, and we quietly took stock of the plates on the table. I caught Sylvie looking curiously at the Sichuan Hot Pot I ordered. I chose it so I could watch her experience it.

"Ever had this?" I asked with a smile. I didn't want her to think I doubted her level of food experience.

"It looks like fondue."

"Close. This is too much here for just me. Will you try it? I haven't had it at this restaurant before."

"Um…okay. But I'll have to take some of mine home, which is totally fine. Nothing better than takeout the next day, right?"

"I couldn't agree more." Finally, we were headed in the right direction.

We focused on our food for a bit. Murmurs of pleasure could be heard. The aromas of garlic and soy sauce filled the air around us.

"Okay, so what do I want to learn about the mysterious Sylvie? Hmmm… Let's start with a softball question. What brought you from Alabama to Virginia?"

"A job." Sylvie tilted her head and frowned. Did she want to say something more? I waited, but she fiddled with the napkin on her lap and avoided eye contact. Her silence highlighted the clinking of silverware around us. Not many folks using the paper-wrapped chopsticks, including my dinner partner.

"No family, boyfriend…to bring you here?" I'm just curious. Authors naturally are.

"No, they're all back in Birmingham."

"Can you tell me about the folks you left behind?"

Okay, yes, I wanted to find out if she had a boyfriend. Perhaps I should not know in case it ruins the whole muse flow, but I opened the door. Eventually, I wanted all the information I could get.

"Well…" She let out the word in a long, heavy sigh, as though her family were exasperating. Or maybe I was. "I have my Momma and Daddy. Plus, my older sister Constance Miller. Grandparents are all gone. Assorted aunts, uncles, and cousins dot the Alabama landscape."

"Wow, I like that phrase."

"What phrase?"

"Dot the Alabama landscape. It's not a phrase people use to describe family members' locations. Just interesting. Words are my business, and I love a good turn of phrase." I shrugged my shoulders because deep frown lines furrowed her forehead. It's not a big deal, I wanted her to know.

"I see. Glad I'm entertaining you."

"Oh boy. I'm sorry, didn't mean to offend."

"Just messing with you. You deserve it. Right?"

I laughed and held up one hand in surrender. My other was holding a fork filled with food I wanted to eat.

"You got me."

Sylvie's satisfied grin faded as she looked around the restaurant. I'd grown used to the low murmurs of patrons and the clanging from the kitchen and had mostly tuned it out.

My gaze followed hers. The other group had left without stopping by. We must have looked engrossed. Sylvie had certainly captured my undivided attention.

"I should probably go." Sylvie bit her bottom lip. Then she tucked that errant hair behind her ear again. I liked it forward.

I caught the server's attention, and we filled our to-go boxes. Neither of us spoke during this process. I think Sylvie was trying to sort through my paying for her dinner. She'd protested, but I won the argument. I owed her a meal since I'd upset her last week. She relented, but refused to engage in eye contact after that. Not quite like a cornered animal, but a little skittish. This wasn't how I wanted our evening to end.

Energy coursed through me. As much as I wanted to keep talking to her, I was desperate to get home and open my laptop. I still hadn't found a way to keep us in the same orbit into the future. How long would I need my muse? I wondered.

"Will I see you at the animal center when I pick up Riley? Assuming my references check out, that is."

"I doubt it. Sunday is my usual volunteer day. You'll have to pick up Riley Monday through Friday."

Man, this wasn't going to plan. I searched for a reason to get her number while we put on our coats and grabbed our food.

She walked to the door ahead of me. Her gray coat's belt draped loosely in the back. It's cold out but not so chilly we had to button up tightly.

"Hey, in case I have an issue with Riley, could I call you?"

I was happy to be talking to her back because that way I'd miss the eye roll or disgusted rejection. I mean, how obvious can a guy be?

"I'm not gonna ask you out or anything. Just dog questions."

I grimaced at how stupid that sounded. Time to roll my eyes at myself.

"I guess so. I can always block you if you're a pain."

That sounded rough, but spoken in that soft southern voice, I felt invited to be blocked. I believed it might be a pleasure.

I had the wisdom not to laugh.

"Sure. Sure. I will not be a pain. Scout's honor."

Chapter 7

Sylvie

I didn't expect Pete to call. Not really. A part of me hoped he would. Just a tiny part.

I found something sweet about him as he sat across from me, eating that spicy food out of the hot pot. His face went a little pink, and with each bite he winced, like he was experiencing extreme pain. I desperately wanted to ask if he intentionally sought out misery at dinner, but that seemed like making fun, which I'd never do with a practical stranger. Instead, I had watched as perspiration beaded on his upper lip.

Angie predicted he would invent a dog disaster so he could call me. She was convinced he was interested.

"Maybe not falling, falling…but, you know, in *like* with you." Angie had giggled into the phone after that middle-school swoon. I swear that girl has always been the most hopeless romantic. She hasn't had a serious boyfriend in three years. Not since Bill Alexander dumped her on Christmas Eve. Honestly, what is wrong with people? We were convinced he was about to propose.

I had been home from Nashville for the holidays, so I spent half of Christmas Day consoling her with hot chocolate and tissues. I sat beside her and dispensed the tissues whenever she tossed one in the tiny straw wastebasket she kept beside the bed in her childhood bedroom.

I hadn't given Pete my number enthusiastically, so I harbored serious doubts that he'd get the courage to hit the call button. That is, assuming he could tell I didn't want to do it. My guy radar hadn't been running on all cylinders lately. Granted, he had courage enough to speak insults to a woman he didn't know. No, I was not yet over that.

Maybe it stings because he turned out to be right. In a way. Online dating may have its merits, but it hadn't been very productive for me. At least not yet. Though I can't say I gave it a real college try. Three dates set up, a repeat, one bust, and one no-show. I promised Angie I'd scroll through more profiles in the new year. I didn't want to enter a third year in Richmond as a single woman. How desperate would I feel in six months, I wondered. My family, Momma in particular, would wonder what's up with me.

It's not like I'm a troll or a rotten date. I've made two positive impressions. Out of two, which is like batting a thousand, right? I don't remember all the sports references I learned in high school. Still…I have to reciprocate the positive feelings, and that's a problem for me. Am I too picky?

The second guy, Jeff, asked to see me again. Apparently, my signal machine wasn't working because I'm pretty sure I sent off a clear "not interested" vibe. Instead of saying an absolutely, positively plain "no" to him, though, I relapsed to my people-pleasing ways. I've put him off until after Christmas. Said I was busy, and I suppose he bought it. He gave me a thumbs-up and that's the last I've heard from him.

Instead of the coffee he'd invited me for, Tim and I

had a second dinner together. Seeing me had inspired him to reconnect with some of his friends back in Birmingham in between our dates. I got some good gossip, basically. Angie was thrilled.

She got a kick out of hearing some new juicy stories. That she's the one who still lives there gave us a few giggles. I pointed out that it's a sign she worked too much. She sighed heavily in agreement.

Gossip doesn't get me excited like it does Momma or Angie. They're just stories about people. I believe stories are important. Very important. But I can't bring myself to get wound up about the daily interactions some people enjoy sharing like they're novelists. The glee they express over a person's unfortunate events is just…I don't know, um…unfortunate?

I'm just saying I'm not going to get all excited about someone's sad drama. Unless it's mine. Or Angie's. I'd go to bat for my best friend. She would do the same for me.

When I worked at the animal shelter again yesterday, Victoria told me that my *friend* had picked up Riley on Friday afternoon.

"That's great!" I said, while filling water bowls in the cages. We wouldn't go out to a pet store for another adoption event until the new year.

"He said you'd agreed to let him call you if he has questions."

"Mm-hmm."

"What're you gonna do if he calls you? Will you go out with him? You both looked pretty cozy at The Kitchen Wok last week."

"Cozy? Oh, I don't know about that. We were just talking." I shrugged, hoping she'd leave me to my work.

"Well, what if he calls—"

"If he calls, it'll be about Riley, not about me."

"Uh, huh. We'll see about that. You'll tell me if he does? Please?"

I nodded and headed to the faucet to turn off the hose.

"He's gonna call."

"We'll see, boss. Now, what else do you need me to do?"

"I see what you did there. Changing the subject. No biggie. We'll have this discussion again."

I blew out a soft breath. I really didn't want to talk about him. The memory of our dinner occupied too many of my lonely moments. Those crinkling eyes and his warm voice distracted me at the most inconvenient times. I hated being so lonely that I'd give into such a ridiculous attraction.

"Let's go review adoption paperwork. You ever done it before?"

"Nope. I'd love to learn."

Victoria kindly stopped talking about Pete. Not that I could stop thinking about him.

****

I couldn't stop wondering about what I'd say if Pete called. I always keep my phone beside me when I'm using my laptop at my "office desk" slash kitchen island. And that's where it usually stays, no matter where I am in this tiny apartment.

But not today. I even took it to the bathroom every time. And downstairs to the mailbox in the entry hall. Eye roll. I'm an eighth grader now.

Thankfully, the phone didn't ring at all during the workday. I couldn't believe, on a Monday, my boss didn't call. But he didn't, and neither did any clients, so I was protected from the nauseating stomach gallops a girl gets when the phone rings and it might be "him." No sweaty palms either.

As I pulled a plate of spaghetti out of the microwave, my phone rang. I'd gotten busy with a project proposal that's due next week, so dinner was later than usual. I was happy to have a serious distraction, so I didn't think about Pete in his hot leather jacket every millisecond.

I nearly dropped the plate to get to my phone. The screen displayed Pete's picture and his name. I grinned. Stupid grinning-grin grins. Then, my insides kinked up like the rubber garden hose used to do in our yard.

I stood up straight and ran my hands through my hair. Like he could see me? I let out a breath.

Answering the call, I said, "Hello?" You know, like I wasn't sure who was calling me.

"Sylvie. I'm so glad you answered. I need some advice."

"Okay. What's up?"

How cool and casual I was as I leaned back against the island.

"Riley, of course. I got him a few days ago. Otherwise, I wouldn't have called. As promised."

"Hey, it's okay. What seems to be the problem?"

"He's hiding in the corner of the hall bathroom. Behind the toilet." Pete sighed. "I can't get him to come out except to eat and drink. He mostly attempts to do that when he thinks I'm not around."

"Hmm. It's good that he's eating and drinking some. Do you think he's getting enough?"

"I've no idea." I imagined Pete was rubbing the top of his head as he said that.

"So, what stuff do you have for him? A bed, dog toys?"

"I don't have any of that. I was going to go with my mom to pick stuff out when I give her Riley for Christmas."

"That's still a few weeks out, Pete. May I suggest you give Riley to your mom early?"

"Well…. I just have this image of a Christmas morning puppy."

"You're describing the reverse of a childhood dream to wake up to a puppy." I laughed.

Pete chuckled. "I guess you're right."

"May I be blunt?"

"Go for it."

"It's a concern that you'll make Riley comfy at your place, and then you'll move him again. If he's already anxious…" I stopped talking when I realized I sounded over-zealous.

"Yeah, yeah. I get it. Okay, lemme think that plan through. But in the meantime, would you mind coming over to check him out? Be sure we're diagnosing the problem correctly."

"Come to your place?" I squeezed my eyes shut. What's wrong with me? Other than being a doofus—my sister's nickname for me. Cute, huh? Clearly, I had hoped Pete would call and now I was nervous or scared or whatever.

"Are you open to that?" Pete's breathing quickened, and I could hear him moving around.

"Sure. Tonight? Um, I just need to wolf down my dinner and I can be over."

"That works. My address is 2750 Floyd Avenue. It's in The Fan."

"Hang on. I'll put it in my GPS and give you a ballpark when I can be there. You're not too far. Okay, yeah, you're about twelve blocks. I'm on Broad Street in The Lofts."

"The VCU housing? You're a student?" His tone sounded accusatory.

"No. I am not a VCU student. But when I moved here eighteen months ago, the university couldn't fill all the units, so they rented out top floor apartments to anyone."

"Hmm. Interesting. So, about what time will you be here?"

I'd already started eating my spaghetti, which was no longer warm enough, but, oh well. Dogs are more important than food.

"Give me thirty minutes."

"See you then. And thank you, Sylvie, for doing this."

"No problem. Speaking of problems, what's the parking situation around your place?"

"Uh, it's The Fan!"

"Okay. I'll figure it out."

"This place is on a corner, so try North Vine Street. It runs beside me, so you may get lucky."

"Okey-dokey. See ya soon." I ended the call and slid my plate back into the microwave for a minute. While that reheated, I ran to the bathroom to brush my hair.

I looked down at my sweatpants and they wouldn't do, so I dug a pair of jeans out of the laundry basket. Nice and soft, they slipped on easily. He'd just have to see the same sweatshirt again.

****

Pete's place wasn't hard to find. I drove past it to get

my bearings, then circled the block. He was right: North Vine Street offered me a decent spot. I parallel parked—thank goodness I learned this required skill in driver's ed—and got out of my car. Its red paint glistened under a streetlamp. Zipping up my black puffy coat, I took in my surroundings and crossed over to Pete's corner.

The house was built of red brick. Fat white columns bordered the front porch that spanned its front. Not that the house was huge. It might have been the mirror image of the house to its left, but the owners of that house had painted the brick a drab khaki color. I wrinkled my nose, being a purist who loved the richness of real brick.

The wooden front door had a huge frosted glass window in it, so I saw the blurry shape of Pete headed my way. He smiled widely as he opened the door. He was wearing jeans and a navy sweatshirt with the letters UVA splashed on the front in white and orange.

"A sight for sore eyes. Thanks, Sylvie. I hope Riley is happier to see you than he is me." Pete's eyes clouded with a pained look.

"All right. Where is the little guy?"

Pete turned around and headed up a hallway that fed off his small entryway. Doors lined the hall. Some were open, others closed. I spotted what might be his kitchen at the far end.

"Hey, Riley. Look who came to visit you?" Pete softened his voice and raised it a pitch as he squatted outside the doorway of the blue-tiled powder room.

Riley appeared as only a tan furball behind the toilet. The tips of his floppy ears folded onto the tile floor.

"Poor thing. Hey, Riley boy, do you remember your friend Sylvie? I came to visit!" I clapped my hands softly.

Riley's eyes tracked back and forth between me and Pete. Both of us were squatted down in the doorway.

I noticed his tail stirring a little. The slightest wag.

I nudged Pete with my elbow and whispered, "Look at his tail."

"Aww. You've saved the day."

"Not so fast," I said, as I scooted a little closer. The toilet was a serious obstacle to getting Riley out by force. I didn't want to do that. I pursed my lips, thinking.

"Okay, Pete. Let's go down the hall. Is that your kitchen at the end? I wonder if he'll follow us. My being here is a change. Dachshunds can be incredibly curious."

"Okay." Pete stood and held out a hand to help me up.

"Thanks." I took it, but quickly pulled my hand away, enjoying the butterflies a little more than I should have. Between his woodsy cologne and incredible brown eyes, the tight bathroom setting was too much to handle, so I backed into the hallway.

Chapter 8

Pete

The confident and knowledgeable version of Sylvie was quite appealing. Her hips swayed as she walked toward my kitchen. I admired the way she filled out her jeans. She wasn't anorexic-looking like the women who flirted with me in my publisher's office.

With her right hand, she gestured to emphasize her points about all things Dachshund. Her voice traveled over her shoulder. Her soft drawl skimmed over me like a silk scarf.

I should be grateful. But I was getting an education I didn't really want. Or need. Those feelings illuminated the saying that no good deed goes unpunished. I just wanted to get my mom a dog. Suddenly, my favorite life motto of "not my circus, not my monkeys" was biting me in the butt.

Riley was the star of my circus. Sylvie had entered the center ring, shining and aglow, and I couldn't help but enjoy the show. More than I should. She's lovely and intelligent. And feeling the velvet of her accent, I wondered what it would sound like wrapped around a whisper in my ear. I groaned silently, my heart skipping a beat.

I've avoided entanglements with women since my divorce five years ago. A long time, for sure. The women I'd dated since Evelyn left were more enthralled with P.J.

Monroe, the writer, than the real Pete. I just wanted to be "Pete" in a woman's heart, but that woman remained elusive.

I'm not sure how one goes about figuring out if another's love was true or merely a false interest in the person in order to enjoy the benefits. It's easier to avoid being on the market because I offered a commercial aspect in some women's eyes. When I resolve to do something, I'm usually successful.

Obviously, the writing problem was a separate thing. Creativity does not obey one's resolve. At least, it never has for me. I cannot will words onto the page.

I have had a very successful writing career as P.J. Monroe. Each of my ten detective novels made it to most of the bestseller lists. Occasionally, my agent and publisher expect more of me than I do. Holding onto the brass ring gets old sometimes and I just want a break. Maybe that's why I got stuck writing number eleven.

We pulled out stools from under the island bar and sat down, halfway facing each other. We watched and listened. I'd left the hallway light on.

"Riley? Wanna come have some dinner?" Sylvie's voice pitched higher and sweeter.

We waited.

"Hey, should I get a blanket or something for Riley to sleep on? You said—"

"I wouldn't do that. Buy an actual dog bed that he can get attached to. He'll mark it with his smells."

"Oh, okay. I feel kinda stupid here." Clearly, I knew absolutely nothing about dogs.

"I doubt you're stupid. Getting a new dog is a learning experience for everyone."

She's beautiful *and* kind. My heart leaped.

Sylvie punched my upper arm lightly. "You're learning things that'll help your mom out, right?"

I nodded and offered her a sheepish grin.

"Should we go out and get him the bed and toys now?"

Sylvie scrunched her face and shook her head. "Probably not a good idea for us both to leave. He'll associate that… Well, scratch that. Actually, it doesn't matter much what he learns here since this isn't his final home."

We shrugged in unison and looked at the empty hallway.

"Let's go. It's getting late and people have to work in the morning."

"Listen, I really appreciate you coming over. I'm sorry to call on a weeknight."

"No worries." Sylvie slid off the stool and looked up at me with a smile. Her skin's quite fair for a southern woman. I was close enough to see a faint sprinkle of freckles dotting her nose and cheekbones.

I rubbed a damp hand down my jeans and jangled my keys.

"Ready?"

She nodded and followed me down the hall. On the way, we peeked in at Riley, who remained hunkered down behind the toilet. The spot looked so uncomfortable.

"Back in a little while, Riley. Don't get into anything."

Sylvie chuckled behind me.

"Bets on whether he's still there when we return?" I asked Sylvie as I swung open the front door. She shrugged.

"My car's to the right." I pointed the keyfob at my car parked at the curb two houses down. Its lights flashed. I opened her door, and she stepped off the sidewalk and slid into the tan leather seat.

"Nice car," Sylvie said as I started the engine.

"Thanks. Bought a couple of years ago." I didn't tell her I got it when book nine became a bestseller. I probably should've mentioned it.

"I thought you had a truck."

"Yep, I do. It's parked a couple of blocks over on a wider street."

"I'd like to have a big yard one day. And no parking problems."

"I hear that."

Sylvie rubbed her palms on her jeans, looked around the car, then out the window. I wondered what she was thinking, but figured I better find out where we should head.

"Recommendations, Sylvie? I haven't bought pet stuff in…well, never."

"Go up to Broad Street. Remember where you met Riley?"

"Yep." I entered the info into my GPS and pulled away. I wasn't wearing a coat, so I found a parking spot to get close to the store Sylvie recommended.

As the doors slid open for us, Sylvie asked, "What's your budget? Cheap? Luxury?"

I laughed.

"Show me what Riley needs and we'll figure it out."

"Right this way, then." Sylvie marched off.

The bed was easy to choose, so we made our way to the toy section. I pushed the cart behind my shopping buddy while she told me about one of her grandmother's dogs, also a Dachshund.

"This is like a dog's Christmas dream!" I held my arms out in mock delight—making her laugh, my aim.

We debated the pros and cons of several toy styles until Sylvie convinced me to buy four toys of various shapes and colors. Seemed like a lot for a tiny dog, but I yielded to her expertise.

We drove home in silence with only the car radio softly playing in the background. I wanted to hum, but Sylvie was preoccupied. Every so often, I caught a glimpse of her reflection in the window. For the second time that night, I wondered what she was thinking.

Sylvie stood facing the street while I unlocked the front door. A bark greeted us as the door swung wide into the entryway. Riley stood in the kitchen doorway. He barked once more, then started running. Sylvie squatted to the floor, saying, "Hey, boy."

While she was untangling her hand from the plastic bag containing the toys, Riley launched into her. He began licking her face. I heard her giggle and then she tipped over.

Sylvie yelped. At first, I thought the noise came from Riley, but when I saw her expression, I knew something was off.

"Whoa!" I picked up Riley from the tangle of her legs and the bag of toys. "What happened?"

Sylvie pushed herself up to sitting position. Her legs stuck out straight, and I had to smile when I caught a glimpse of her Santa socks.

"Oh, gosh. Ouch!" She held up her left arm and looked at me with a pained expression.

I put Riley down on the wood floor and muttered, "Stay."

The poor dog looked at Sylvie, licked her hand, and trotted back to the bathroom.

"Let's get you to the kitchen so I can look at your hand."

"I can't put any weight on it."

It took two tries, but we got her standing. We made a lot of noise, and it became obvious that Sylvie was in loads of pain.

"Will you let me slip off your coat? I'll go slow. Promise."

She squinted with pain and nodded.

Once her arms were free, I compared the swelling of her left hand against the right. She couldn't bend her fingers without hissing out her breath.

"Okay. I'm gonna call a buddy of mine. He's a doc." I made the call, all the while watching Sylvie's face. She gently poked her arm in spots from her elbow to her wrist, wincing with nearly every touch. I feared she'd broken it, but what did I know? Hence, my call to Doctor Dave, a friend since college.

I left the kitchen to talk to Dave about Sylvie's injury. He had me return to her so I could accurately describe the swelling and skin color.

"ED?" I looked at my watch and grimaced at Sylvie. Her gray eyes grew enormous, and she shook her head. "All right, Dave. Thanks. I'll let you know how it goes."

As I hung up the phone, Sylvie started blubbering.

"I can't go to an Emergency…" She sniffled. "I hate those places."

"Hey, no one loves them. I'm afraid you may have a break, so a visit to the hospital is required. Do you want me to help you with your coat, or just put it around your shoulders?"

"Shoulders," she mumbled. I hustled to my bedroom and got a box of tissues for the ride.

"You should put Riley's bed down before we go." Even in pain, this sweet woman was thinking of a dog. I shook my head.

While Sylvie stood bravely by the front door, I ripped open the bed's packaging. We disagreed over where it should go for the evening. Sylvie's idea to leave it outside the bathroom won. I feared I'd trip over the thing when I got home later that night. A useless fear since I didn't get home that night at all.

Chapter 9

Sylvie

Pete was great at helping me get into his car. The pain made my body stiff, so I found it difficult to slide in leading with my hurting arm, so he held on to me as I eased in inches at a time. Then he covered me with my coat like it was a blanket.

He winked at me as he adjusted it. His face was inches from mine, so I closed my eyes and held my breath.

As he started the car, he looked at me and asked, "Ready?"

I shook my head and moaned, "I really don't want to go. Bad, bad…"

"Am I correct in assuming you have hospital experience?" He pulled into the street. At nine on a Monday night, the traffic was negligible.

"Mmm, yes." Removing my right hand from under my coat, I dabbed a tissue under my eyes.

"Tell me about it."

"Car accident when I was sixteen."

"You weren't driving, I hope." He looked over and frowned.

"No. Older boys. I don't wanna talk about it."

"What kind of injuries—"

So stubborn, and deaf, too. I interrupted him with a heavy sigh, hoping he'd drop it. But, of course, he kept asking.

"Seriously, look, I'm trying to distract you. Maybe this is the wrong subject at the wrong time. Yeah." He wiped a hand down his face.

"Thank you," I whispered. Strangely, relief flowed when the bright red emergency sign appeared ahead. Somewhere along the ride, maybe I'd surrendered to dealing with doctors and nurses.

"How 'bout I drop you at the door so you can check in? I'll park."

Perspiration beaded on my upper lip as panic seized me. My wrist began to throb in double-time like a mallet was pounding. I couldn't go in there alone.

"No. I'd rather go in with you." I looked at him, desperation likely radiating from my eyes. Understanding flashed across his face, he gradually edged the car to the left lane to get into the deck.

The walk from the parking deck was brutal. The temperature was in the forties, but it felt like below zero without my coat on correctly. I didn't understand why each step I took caused pain to shoot up and down my forearm.

"Do you want me to put my arm around you or hold your good elbow?" I could feel Pete studying me as we walked the short distance to the entrance. He was very attentive, but I wasn't feeling that kindly toward him. He hadn't caused this, but I was too scared to feel grateful.

"I'm good."

"You don't look good, Sylvie. How much pain are you in? On a scale from one to ten? They'll ask you that in here."

I stopped to catch my breath. The pain sapped my energy.

"Right now, it's a six. I wanna sit down."

"Got it."

After he hustled me through the sliding doors, Pete got me to a seat in a bank of nondescript chairs against a wall. He left me there to talk to the admissions desk and returned pretty quickly. A hopeful sign.

"Do you need my help with this?" His voice forced me to open my eyes. Pete held up a clipboard. I should have probably saved him the trouble, but my brain was fear-soaked mush at that point.

"If you don't mind," I breathed out in between spasms.

We weren't finished with the forms when they finally called me back. Pete hesitated. I tilted my head, so he'd know to follow. He stood and took my right elbow. The caring look in his eyes made my throat tighten. Tears were a blink away, so I kept my eyes wide open. Honestly, all I wanted to do was curl into a ball and cry-scream this pain away.

A wave of nausea curled through my chest. I pressed my lips together and blinked. A tear dripped out of my left eye.

"Almost there," said the nurse we were following. I kept his blue scrubs in my periphery while my eyes focused on the floor. Fighting the pain and nausea proved to be a test I hadn't taken for a long time.

Once I was settled on a bed, the nurse took my vitals. Because I wore a sweatshirt, he wanted me to change into a gown. Pete stepped outside while Jason helped me. Jason's expression was noncommittal when he examined my forearm.

"Pete, you can come back in," I called out. I wanted him there when a doctor arrived. I wouldn't be able to talk about the fall.

"Hey, Jason says the doctor's in the next room. You're next." He smiled and gave me two thumbs-up.

A smile swam across my lips.

"Will you talk to him…or her? I can't…talk."

"Absolutely. I'm here for you. Gosh, I'm so sorry this happened. I'm responsible. I'll make it up to you. Just name it."

I closed my eyes to stop his chatter. I breathed deeply and tried to focus on anything but the humming pain in my arm.

It didn't take long before the doctor showed up. He was certain I had a clean break, no broken skin. An x-ray was required for a final diagnosis. So we waited for a technician. Pete's hand visited the top of his head a million times. On his sweatshirt, he wore a sticker with my last name, Bradley, and my room number. Kinda cute.

I hurt, but I wasn't dead. I noticed how the shadow of his beard made him look younger. Though in the fluorescent light, I was sure I saw silver sprinkled in his facial hair, too. We didn't talk, so our little square space filled with the sound of beeping machines and chatter from the hallway.

When the technician collected me for the x-ray, Pete stood and watched as I moved to a wheelchair. I decided he wanted to say something; instead he managed to look a little lost. He was out of his element, I thought.

He held up a hand and said, "I'll be here when you get back."

"Okay" was all I could manage. I wanted this night over. I wanted my bed. Snuggling with my fuzzy Christmas blanket would make me all better.

I found Pete texting when I returned from the radiology department, but he set his phone down to help me out of the wheelchair. The dark-haired nurse aide watched with her hands resting on the chair's handles. I was ready to lie down on the bed, even if it was only a thick, inflexible plastic rubbery material covered by a thin white sheet.

I groaned and rubbed my hand back across the top of my head. Pete's attention snapped to my face, and his eyes roamed across my forehead and right temple.

"Sylvie."

"Yes?"

"Your scars. Um—"

"The car accident, yeah."

I've worked with hair stylists for years to shape thick bangs to curve across my forehead and along my temples. The style's a bit dated, but I've grown to love it. It makes me feel more confident, like nothing else has for over half my life. My scars are ugly and when I see them, I feel ugly. My face was ruined in that accident. And so was my senior year.

I smoothed my hair back over my forehead while avoiding Pete's gaze.

"Will you hand me a tissue? Please." I closed my eyes, lids like dams holding back tears from a well that wouldn't run dry.

I heard Pete opening the tiny box of tissues. He didn't say anything for minutes. Surely, he'd been turned off by that lumpy mess on my face. Why did I care what he thought? I shouldn't, but I did.

"Here." Pete handed me a tissue and set the box on my thigh.

"Where's the doctor? I want to go home. I need

painkillers. You need to check on Riley."

Pete laughed.

At that very moment, the doctor rushed into the room. "Okay, Miss Bradley. You have a hairline fracture in your wrist. Do you want to see your scans?"

I shook my head.

"All right. We're going to splint your wrist—"

"No cast?" I interrupted.

"Not necessary unless it doesn't heal well. But…I am curious. The scan shows some other fracture history."

I put my right hand over my eyes for a moment. This constant reliving of the past tonight had to end.

"I was in a car accident when I was sixteen."

"Right. Well, those fractures probably weakened your bone permanently. Explains tonight's fracture, because a woman your age shouldn't have broken a bone in the fall you described."

I glanced at Pete, but he was hyper-focused on the doctor. Then he asked questions.

"So, you're going to splint it and send her home? Are you sending her home with a pain reliever?"

"Yes, she'll go home tonight, and I'll prescribe an NSAID for pain. You can take that till it's gone or switch to an over-the-counter one, like ibuprofen." The doctor looked between the two of us, waiting for a question.

"Let's do this," I said, unwilling to stay there any longer than necessary.

The doctor stood up from the rolling stool, which bounced against the white cabinet. He nodded at both of us as he slid open the glass door of my room.

"The nurse will be in shortly. I hope you heal well and I'll see you in my office in a couple of weeks. Good night."

I raised my right hand halfway off the bed, and Pete said, "Thanks, Doc."

Of course, it took longer than I wished to escape the place, but by two in the morning, a nurse was wheeling me through the sliding glass exit doors. Pete stood by the open passenger door, grinning. For what reason, I couldn't figure. Maybe he thought he was some co-conspirator in my supposed escape.

"Your chariot awaits."

Oh brother, he went there. I stared straight into the car so I wouldn't roll my eyes.

The pain relievers the hospital gave me dulled my wrist's throbbing. Exhaustion, though, brought on a headache and incredibly dry eyes. My eyes were sore and red from crying, too. I felt like a helpless, hurting child and I wanted my momma. I took a shaky breath to stop the tears from coming again.

Slipping between my cotton sheets could not happen soon enough. We were only about ten minutes from my apartment at this hour.

"How fast can you drive this fancy sports car?" I asked Pete, eyes closed against the streetlights.

"You know, it would help if you looked where we are going."

"My address is in GPS, right?"

"I'm on my own, got it." Pete drummed the steering wheel to the soft rock playing quietly. The wood and spice of his cologne teased my nose.

Pete took me to my apartment. Hilarity ensued when Pete tried to help me get ready for bed. He pulled off my shoes. My Santa socks were the only cheerful part of me. Then, while helping with my jeans, he sort of closed his eyes. After he went back to the living room, I struggled one-handed to pull on some sweats. Needless to say, I planned to sleep in my sweatshirt.

I met Pete back in the kitchen, where he was rummaging through the stuff from the hospital.

"How 'bout I set out some of your pills and a glass of water for you to take through the night?"

"You're not staying?"

He shook his head.

"Riley, remember? The reason you're in this unfortunate situation."

"I know. I was just teasing."

"That's a good sign." He smiled. The island's pendant lamp cast a shimmer in his eyes. Warm fuzziness flowed through me; I was touched he cared so much about my circumstance. I was less alone all of a sudden. I liked that he accepted a place in my support system.

"I'm tired as all-get-out." I yawned out the words. Then yawned again noisily.

"Gee. I get the message." He turned toward the door.

"Wait. Um. Just in case, um, I dunno, I need you? For something medical like. Can I call?"

"Naturally. I'm happy to help in any way."

I opened a kitchen drawer and rummaged around. I found the spare key card for the building security pad.

"So…I guess since you're not a weirdo, you may need this. If I need you, that is." I handed him the key card. I hoped I hadn't sounded harsh with the "weirdo" stuff. He'd been so kind and caring, but I couldn't find the words to take it back.

He stared at it. Mute. I rushed to fill the silence.

"It's my building key card. So I don't have to come down to let you in. Assuming you come over, it's cuz I feel like crap. Right?"

He nodded, thoughtful. "Appreciate your trust. But you're about to fall over. Go to bed." He pointed toward my bedroom with a stern look on his face.

"Good night, Pete. Thanks for taking me to the hospital."

"Of course. It's what chivalrous Pete does. His mother raised him right, you know?"

"You're a good son, then. Lessons don't always stick." I yawned again and walked woozily toward my beckoning bed. I never heard my front door close.

Chapter 10

Pete

Riley the Rotten Dog was sleeping in the middle of the hallway on the new bed. Score one for Sylvie. He lifted his head as I opened the front door and dropped it again with a soft murmur. Do dogs murmur? That's what it sounded like. At least, I didn't feel scolded.

Riley didn't deserve scolding, though he had tinkled in the kitchen. That's not his fault. I squatted down to pet him, and he rolled on his back for a belly rub. Yahoo! I was not too tired to be excited about this development. I couldn't wait to tell Sylvie that we have progress.

We? What am I thinking? There's no "we" here. But she did actually feel like a member of the Pete-n-Riley team.

"C'mon, boy. Let's go sniff the back yard. And do your business."

I shivered on the back stoop while Riley sniffed the fence. The porch lighting was poor quality, but I was pretty sure he did something. I could sleep without worrying about more puddles.

Puddle. I had to take care of the current one before bed. My eyes burned with weariness. Long day, and little to report on the writing front. Make that *nothing* to report. I'd spent the day worrying over Riley, then called Sylvie.

The rest of my life was one big adventure.

Sometime after four in the morning, I fell asleep wondering if Sylvie was doing okay. Riley woke me at seven. Nothing I tried kept him quiet, so I wearily climbed into yesterday's jeans. I threw a brown plaid flannel shirt over a beige T-shirt and declared myself ready for Tuesday.

I opened the door to let out Riley and discovered a brilliant sun and frigid air. I watched Riley explore the tiny back yard through the kitchen window while I made coffee. Strong brew was required by this very sleepy man. The earthy aroma was almost enough to awaken my brain—almost enough.

Riley came back in and headed straight to his bowl, which was empty. He'd eaten all of it while I was with Sylvie, little bugger. He did seem to be acting less scared. I figured I'd wait a few days before I declared the problem solved, though.

Then again, it'll be Mom's problem. Sylvie had urged me to give Riley to Mom sooner rather than later. I sipped my strong black coffee and leaned against the kitchen counter. Bare branches swayed lightly in the winter breeze. I wouldn't forget my coat today.

Should I call Sylvie to check on her?

I grabbed my phone and shot her a text: "u like coffee?"

Immediately, the phone vibrated in my hand. "Yes, pls."

I looked in the hallway mirror and saw a man wearing a ridiculous grin. And an extremely ugly shirt. Geez Louise, man.

Sylvie opened her door wearing the same red sweatshirt and gray sweats. I was walking into another adventure, I reckoned.

"How'd you sleep?" I asked as I set down the cardboard cupholder and pastry bag on her island.

She shrugged and ran a hand through her hair. Just remembering she hadn't brushed it, I thought. The shiny pink skin of her forehead scars peeked through cowlicked bangs. I wanted to trace a finger over them.

"Okay, I guess. I kinda passed out when you left. I woke up once and took more meds. It was still dark then. I got up after you texted me."

I handed her a coffee without the travel lid. The fingers on her left hand were swollen and dark pink. She closed her eyes and breathed in the aroma, just like I do every morning.

"How's Riley?" She slurped her coffee.

I gestured at the pastry bag and raised my eyebrows in question.

"Yes, yes. And this coffee is fantastic."

"I got it from Morris Street Cafe." I smirked.

"Ha-ha." She pointed to the donut with pink frosting and sprinkles. I found her a plate in the second cabinet I opened. It was white with a red pattern on the edge. Christmasy.

"You haven't answered about Riley. Is something wrong?" Worry creased the space between her eyebrows.

"Nothing's wrong at all. Here's the full report. He peed in the kitchen. Was sleeping on the bed you picked out when I got home last night. This morning, I mean. He went out in the back yard. Let me go to bed. Woke me when the sun came up. Went outside again. Ate breakfast. Was sleeping on his bed when I left."

"No hiding in the bathroom, then?"

I shook my head.

"Huh. Interesting."

71

"Yeah, definitely. Especially him eating in front of me. Odd, right?"

"I guess so."

"It's like you cast a magic spell before he broke your arm."

Sylvie rolled her eyes and looked down at her splint.

"I know you have to work, but could you do a couple of things before you go?" She gazed around the room like she was making a list.

"Sure thing. What do ya need?"

"Um, I think I'll work in bed today. So I need my laptop plugged in there." She gestured toward the living room, where her laptop rested on a glass-and-chrome coffee table. The whole apartment was sleek and mostly gray. It didn't match her, to my mind.

Except for all the plants by the window! Interesting. A question for another day.

I did her bidding, setting up the laptop so she could sit against her headboard and pillows and type to her heart's content. I caught sight of the skimpy red top she'd worn to the cafe two weeks ago, draped over a chair in the corner. Black heels leaned at an angle against each other beneath the chair. I left the room, uncomfortable with the depth of my curiosity.

"What if you made a basket of bottled water for me? I'm trying to fix my bedroom so I can stay there most of today. I feel like you-know-what."

I quirked an eyebrow at that last remark. She doesn't swear?

"Okay, what about food? If you're taking prescription painkillers, it shouldn't be on an empty stomach."

"Okay, Dr. Pete! Look at you all caregiving…"

I rolled my eyes and pulled water out of her stainless-steel refrigerator.

"Crackers, snacks?"

Sylvie pointed to the cabinet door to the right of the stove vent hood. I held out a bag of cheese crackers shaped like fish.

"Do you entertain toddlers too?"

"Hey! Not nice. I love those. And yes, I will eat them. I think I have grapes in the fridge."

"What are you gonna do about showering?"

"I don't need any help, if that's what you're asking."

My face grew warm. I held up both hands, palms facing out. "Not where I was going."

She was blushing too. Yet her gray eyes were watery and tired. She was in more pain than she was letting on.

"What if I wrap your arm in a plastic bag before I go? You should be able to manage a good rinse at least. It'll make you feel better, too."

"Okay, let's try that. See if I can remove it on my own. But first I have to get this sweatshirt off. Geez Louise."

I chuckled.

"What?"

"I say 'Geez Louise' too. Funny."

"Yeah, funny weird."

I shook my head and gestured her over to me. I helped her ease the sweatshirt sleeve over the bandage. She hissed quietly when her arm jiggled too much. How she dealt with pain was impressive.

"Why the heck did I put this back on over this bandage last night?"

"Maybe the freezing night air?"

She shrugged. After a few attempts, I got her

bandaged arm waterproofed. At least I hoped it would work.

"I'm headed to the shower. Will you see yourself out? I don't want to walk to the door half-dressed, you know?"

I didn't comment on the half-dressed remark. Her red Alabama sweatshirt angled across her shoulders and, with her good arm, she held the bulk of it down over her chest. I could make out the edge of a beige bra that shimmered in the kitchen light.

"Text me if you need anything."

Sylvie nodded.

"I mean it. Anything at all."

"I will." She walked backward to her bedroom.

"And be careful."

She shot me a thumbs-up and closed the door. Its black paint delivered a clear message that I was banned from there.

I cleaned up our breakfast stuff and then surveyed her plants. They made up quite a collection. Some were partially blocked from view by a long box, which I nudged with my foot. A Christmas tree. I turned in a full circle and noted a red plastic bin with the word "Christmas" written in black on the lid.

I wanted to linger to make sure Sylvie made it out of the shower safely, but I quit my snooping and left.

I had writing to do. Not that I got to it right away. Riley greeted me at the front door with a toy. He'd figured out how to bite it to make it squeak. Sylvie probably picked that one on purpose. There's a bit of mischief about her. I liked that. But I didn't like the way she fascinated me in ways my wife never had.

Perhaps Twain was right. Familiarity breeds

contempt. "And children" is the rest of the quote. Thank goodness Evelyn and I never had kids. She wasn't the nurturing type. I'm not saying I'm prize parent material either. Growing up with a single mom, I didn't have an actual father figure to emulate, though I experienced a couple of male stand-ins. Mom sure was a great parent, though. She didn't miss a trick—always there for my games and school stuff. I was one of the lucky ones.

I took Riley for a walk on the new leash we bought last night. Lime green dogs covered the navy-blue leash. Kinda preppy-looking, which made me smile at Sylvie's choice again. Riley's short legs took us two blocks and back. I wasn't winded, but he was. He stood over the bowl and lapped up water for minutes.

His chocolate puppy-dog eyes teased me into giving him a treat. Next thing I knew, Riley plopped onto the bed, still in the middle of the hallway, and sighed heavily.

While I typed in the dining room, Riley's light snores maintained a quiet rhythm. I stared at the berries outside my window, reminded once again of Sylvie's top the first day I saw her.

I was already three-quarters through my initial draft, the synopsis sent off yesterday before I called Sylvie. I had held that back because I hated creating expectations for my publisher. For one thing, characters sometimes have their own stories to tell, and a story summary developed too early can become untrue—its own fiction.

Carol can be a Pitbull, but she's sweet most of the time. Demanding Carol has been the model for a few book characters over the years—not that she's picked up on that. How many of us see ourselves that clearly, anyway?

Writing so many words in two weeks was unusual for me. Long nights, little sleep, and my muse, Sylvie, had been a winning combo. The story had existed in my head, but it just wouldn't come out through my fingertips. It took Sylvie to crash the dam that held me back. Not meeting her, just seeing her, and hearing that soft southern syrup in her voice had been mythical indeed.

Sylvie existed in my head a little more than I wanted while I wrote. I wondered if I'd get even more words on the page when I quit daydreaming about her. While helping her undress, I discovered her skin was smooth and pale as alabaster. *While helping her undress*...I wish I could say that in another context, one where we're together and—

I had to get back to work, but my imagination had run in absolutely the wrong direction for a crime-thriller writer. Sylvie had gotten too far in my head, even though I didn't know exactly how this muse thing worked. I knew I had to focus on the words.

What was it about her? When we parted ways after this brief interlude, would I be able to finish this book without her?

My phone was silent the entire day, keeping me focused. Sylvie hadn't reached out. Did that mean she was doing okay? What if she fell in the shower after I left? I wondered if she had any family around.

"Hey, do you have anyone to help nearby?" The text message sent with a whoosh.

Three dots appeared on my screen, then vanished. Then she was back. I waited, thinking she was sending a text-novel.

"No. In Alabama."

She must've deleted half her message. Or maybe she's being overly cautious with me.

"I'm bringing you dinner," my text said.

Dots came and went. She's indecisive. I liked that and I didn't know why.

I saved my work and grabbed my jacket. Riley looked at me from his bed.

"Dang, fella. C'mon, you gotta do some business outside." I hooked on his leash, and we were out the front door; he trotted ahead of me. He was one laid-back pup. I could get attached.

Strange. I'd successfully avoided attachments for five years. I'm falling for a dog and…

I stopped on the sidewalk and shook my head fiercely. "Snap out of it, Monroe."

Chapter 11

Sylvie

When Pete said he was bringing dinner, my tummy dropped like I was on a roller coaster. Part excitement, part anxiety about being with him after last night at the hospital and again this morning. He saw me at my worst, and he's not my type. Granted, I've not dated enough to know the kind of guy who's best for me. Can anyone really know? That's a stupid question that most married people would answer, "of course you can know, Dodo bird!"

My dating history has been rather limited for a thirty-two-year-old. When I mention that I was a cheerleader and a majorette, the eyebrows go up, and assumptions run rampant. Uh, no. I'm actually still a virgin. Surprised?

You and me both.

I suppose I have always been too particular. And guarded. When I let my guard down in college and dated my roommate's brother, Danny, for a year, I learned some painful lessons. Don't mix friendship, family, and dating. I loved my roomie, Mariah, but after our sophomore year, we no longer hung out. I lost a great roommate and dear friend because I dated her older brother, who turned out to be a horrible jerk.

For some reason, she didn't enjoy witnessing my fury at her brother's rottenness. I overheard his friends joking about my scars and Danny laughed and murmured, "Yeah," or something like that. I was so hurt. Finally, after three painful years, I had felt attractive again, but not even my boyfriend appreciated me enough to stand up for me. The Sylvie of ten years ago wanted him to punch the terribly rude friend—lights out.

Since then, nothing's ever felt quite right. Perfection is a loser's game, I've always believed, but my standards won't lower when it involves planning my future life with a man. I absolutely, positively can't fall in love with someone like Daddy.

Oh, he's charming, all right. Momma graduated top of her high school class, but she didn't go any further. She fell for a handsome future lawyer, had two girls, and the rest is an imperfect history. I reckon Momma's always been happy enough. Our house felt tinged with disappointment, though, like the drapes drooped a little and cobwebs threatened to bring down the dining room chandelier.

Pete. He's charming too, which makes me wanna turn tail and run. Fast, with no cartwheel interruptions. Just make a beeline elsewhere. Anywhere but a place where I fall for a kind man.

A kind man I knew little about. Perhaps tonight, over dinner—I wondered what he was bringing—I could find out more of his story. My head may want to run, but my heart was conspiring against me. I wanted to know more about the fascinating and extremely handsome Pete Monroe. I was all mushy inside.

Tim texted me today while I was talking to my boss on a video call. He wanted to go out a third time. I told him I'd just broken my wrist and I wasn't up to making plans right now. He was sympathetic, sweetly offering to bring me fast food for lunch. I passed, of course. I was in no condition to entertain.

Oddly, I didn't think of Pete coming over with dinner as entertaining. Hmm. I wondered briefly what that meant, but I wasn't ready to analyze my life. Or my feelings.

My heart skipped a beat when Pete knocked on my door an hour after he'd promised dinner. He's a man of his word, I'd learned in the past two weeks. I couldn't decide if that was enough to override his questionable ability to pay his bills.

I brushed my hair right after he said he was coming over. Brushed my teeth. Pinched my cheeks for color, but when that didn't work on my extreme pallor, I brushed on a little rosy blush. I still looked rough, I thought. My eyes were tinged with exhaustion and discomfort.

I smelled garlic and soy the minute I opened the front door. Pete held up a brown paper bag and announced, "I went back to the Kitchen Wok for our dinner."

"Yum," I said as I backed away and let him in.

"I stuck with mostly the same order we had, um…how long ago did we eat there? I lose track of time when I'm deep in a project. The holidays don't help either."

I led Pete to the kitchen island and got plates out of the cabinet. He unpacked the food and the scent of it made my mouth water.

Pete hummed while he worked.

"What's that song?"

"No Show Jones." He grinned wickedly.

I frowned. "What's that supposed to mean?"

"There was this country western singer, George

Jones, and sometimes he'd drink a little too much and never make it to the stage. Hence the nickname and the song."

"Ohhhh." I scratched my nose, trying to hide my amusement.

"Did you ever get an explanation from the guy who stood you up?"

I rolled my eyes. "Really?"

Pete held up his hands in surrender. "I apologize. Not my business."

"I was ghosted."

"Ghosted? What's that mean?"

"Are you messing with me?"

He shook his head.

"You seriously don't know what it means? Wow! You sleep in a crypt?"

I laughed when he ran his hand through his hair.

"How old are you, Sylvie? Let's level set us." He pointed between the two of us.

Us. My brain sizzled. Fear and happiness mingled together. I felt a pull toward him I didn't think I could name. Or didn't want to admit to. My throat thickened as I started to talk, like my heart was clogging it up.

"I turned thirty-two in October."

"I'll be forty-one in January," Pete said as he spooned fried rice onto our plates.

"That's not old." I scooped rice into my mouth.

"Thank you. Appreciate the kind words."

I rolled my eyes at him again.

"That eye-roll thing is a bit middle school, don't you think?" He winked at me, so I knew he was just kidding. I changed the subject and didn't point out the obvious age difference. When I was in middle school wasn't he in college?

"Why aren't you married? At your age." I winked back at him, but his expression darkened.

"I was. Divorced five years. Not the best chapter of my life."

"I'm sorry. I've never been married or close to it."

"Hmm."

"Tell me about your mom. Does she live around here?"

"Yes, my mom lives in the West End. She is getting close to retirement from being a hospital nurse."

"Now I know where you get it."

"Get what?"

"The caregiving thing. I don't know what I would have done without you yesterday and today."

"First, you wouldn't have a broken wrist." Pete snorted and shook his head.

"Be that as it may, you've been a hero. And gone above and beyond."

Pete's face flushed pink, and he looked down at his plate. I wondered what he was thinking. My apartment would have been silent, except I could hear laughter coming from the television in my bedroom. Sitcoms had been my background noise all day while I tried to work.

"So, how was your day today? Did you get any work done one-handed?"

"Ha. Right." I shook my head in dismay. "I talked to my mom and Angie. I also talked to my boss." I was about to roll my eyes and thought better of it.

"Did you get a suitable amount of sympathy?"

"From the ladies, yes, but not from Patrick. He's insisting I keep an appointment with a client on Thursday. I just don't think I will be able to drive yet."

"I'll take you."

"No. Wait. Why?" He didn't feel that guilty about my wrist, did he?

"Well, you need help. And I'm here." Pete sat up straight and tall, smiling, like I had a choice between him and some other handsome guy. There I go again with the handsome thing. I stared at him; lusted, actually. Who wouldn't imagine her fingers in that dark wavy hair and—

Geesh. I should reconsider how much time I can spend with this man and stay sane.

"It's only ten minutes from here. I suppose I could call a rideshare."

"You'd choose a stranger over me? Thanks a lot."

"Oh no! I didn't mean it that way. I can't keep infringing on your time. Don't you have a job?"

"I'm kinda self-employed."

Right. I wanted to ask him about that, but was afraid to hear the whole truth about his sketchy employment. So much about him didn't make much sense—the cool car, the truck, the small apartment, his loosey-goosey work hours.

"Sylvie, tell me about your family."

I groaned inside. I've never crafted a short story version of my lineage. "It's complicated" doesn't begin to cover my family's miserable tale. Or tales, plural, if you add Daddy's little fictions.

I blew out my breath.

"My family, huh? Just remember, you asked."

"Got it." Pete snickered.

"Momma comes from one of the 'First Families of Birmingham' and she's the source of our supposed wealth."

"Wait. First family? What's that?"

"Oh, you know, people who can trace family members back to the settling of the city. Stuff like that."

"Didn't know it was a thing."

I pointed my fork at him and squinted.

"How long have you been in Richmond?"

"Most of my life."

"Building names, streets, stuff like that. Do your research, and you'll find a list of first families here too."

"I stand corrected." Pete stood then and started clearing our dishes.

"Are you headed home?"

"No. Just cleaning up. You haven't finished your family story. I'm curious about your supposed wealth." He wiggled his eyebrows, and I laughed.

He's not rude. Another good mark for him.

"There is no money, or very little. Just a gorgeous old house that always needs fixing. It's the age-old story, right?"

"Right." Pete continued to put dishes in the dishwasher. White take-out boxes went into my fridge.

I figured he didn't know what I meant but was just agreeing with me.

"Anyway, I have a sister, Constance Miller Bradley Williams. She's married, no kids yet. They've been trying for a while, I think. Momma's dying for a grandchild, preferably a girl she can frilly all up."

Pete smiled and leaned his elbows on the counter. His face was twelve inches from mine across the cool granite.

"Tell me more."

"Not sure what to tell. I can think of a lot to leave out." I was so tired, even though it was only eight o'clock. I laughed and hid a yawn behind my bandaged arm.

"Another time. You're beat. I can see it around your eyes. Even if you didn't yawn in my face."

Thank heavens I didn't have to discuss my family that night. He even had good radar. Or maybe he was just bored.

"I appreciate the dinner. This was sweet of you."

"I like your company. I still don't know what you do for a living, and all that."

"Same here." I yawned again. At that point, I couldn't be less curious about his job, or lack thereof.

Pete slipped on his leather jacket and started toward the door.

"I'll text you tomorrow night about your Thursday work appointment. Okay?"

"K" was all I could croak out. My throat had tightened. I started missing him as he put on his jacket. I stayed on the stool and waited for the door to close.

My arm began to throb. I hadn't felt any pain while Pete was here.

My phone pinged with a text message. It was from Pete. Did he forget something?

"I saw your Christmas decorations by the window. Don't try doing it alone. I'm happy to help you on the weekend. Ok?"

Man. This guy was going the extra-extra. What would Angie have to say about these developments? Oh, I know.

Texting was awkward and slow with a broken wrist, so I used voice-to-text to reply.

"Sure, Pete. That's sweet. I figured I'd never get to it this year. I'm free all weekend, of course."

Dots appeared on the screen. I waited impatiently for his response.

"Wow, that was fast for a gal with a bad arm."

"Voice to text," I said back.

"Huh?"

"Never mind." He's pretty hopeless on that front.

"Good night, Sylvie. Sweet dreams."

"Same."

He sent back a laughing emoji, the one with the tears.

In bed, I thought about my family, all the parts I didn't want to tell Pete. You see, a lot of my family story is like a costume party. People wear masks or they just say everything's okay while wearing cute outfits. When I was little, I didn't understand much, of course. Thank goodness I didn't know that Daddy never passed the Bar. And thank goodness my elementary school friends didn't know any better than I did. I believed I was special, being a lawyer's kid. I'm still embarrassed when I reflect on that time in my life.

He worked at the courthouse. That part was true. Somewhere in a filing room, he spent his days concocting reasons to slip out a back door and lose a few dollars at the track.

Maybe that's why he acted slightly amused and a bit proud when he learned I'd been sneaking out of the house to meet up with Angie and other friends back in ninth grade. But the summer before my senior year, I saw no amused glint in his eye when he found out I'd gone somewhere I shouldn't have. Later in adulthood, I wondered if Daddy had enjoyed the brief reprieve from being the sole troublemaker in our house.

I'd been wearing my seatbelt in the backseat of an

old green Pontiac Catalina. Doug, a sweaty football player from another school, sat between Angie and me. Two guys sat up front: Jake and Billy. When we swerved into a grove of peach trees, bouncing all over the rutted ground, all three of us in the back slid to the right, crushing my head against the broken window glass. Doug's body crushed my left side, breaking a rib and my forearm in two places. He and Angie suffered minor cuts and bruises. My favorite lime-green top was ruined by all the blood. Jake, another football player, was driving drunk. We both went to the hospital in ambulances, but I never saw him again. Someone worked it out so I didn't have to go to court months later when Jake had to appear.

Those stupid boys from one county over could've ruined our lives completely, but we avoided a greater calamity. Five teenagers driving wild and only two of us ended up in the hospital.

We were lucky. At least that's what the cops said. But that accident changed my senior year in the most disappointing ways.

Chapter 12

Pete

Taxi driver is not a job I've ever aspired to. But there I was waiting outside a building, watching for a beautiful woman in a gray coat to come out the door.

Sylvie's text had asked me to pull up out front—in a no-parking zone, no less, but there I sat, fiddling with the radio dial. I wondered what music she liked. Movement caught my eye and Sylvie appeared, pushing her good side against the glass door.

With catlike grace, I hopped out of the car and opened her door.

"Thanks." She smiled at me and slid down into the leather seat.

"Good morning. You ready for this?"

Sylvie sighed. "I begged Patrick to let me hold this meeting by phone or video. But they have contractual issues to discuss. He's right; they're better worked out in person." She patted the zippered leather portfolio on her lap.

"How's your wrist?" I pulled out into traffic once I caught a traffic break. Rush hour downtown is not my favorite time to be out and about. Yet another great thing about the writing life, I'm not forced onto the nine-to-five hamster wheel. Though explaining myself to my agent sometimes feels like I'm working way too hard to avoid flying off that spinning cage.

"You ever break a bone?"

I shook my head.

"This is my fourth. I broke my right thumb in a cheering incident." She wiggled her thumb.

"Cheering incident, huh?"

"I'm in no mood to describe. Dumb kid luck is all."

"But wait…four broken bones?"

She sighed, and expecting a lengthy tale, I interrupted.

"Hold that thought. Where're we going?"

"Seventh and Franklin. Any corner'll do."

"Got it. Okay. So…broken bones?"

"Right. Well, I mentioned the accident." She touched her bangs on the right side, away from my view.

"It was a drunk driving incident, not me. We were joy riding out in the country. I ended up with a broken rib, two broken bones in my arm. You know, the ones the doctor mentioned on Monday night."

She looked over at me. I took my eyes off the road for a second to give her a small sympathetic smile.

"Tough time, I guess?"

"Yep. It happened the summer before my senior year. I was going to be the majorette captain in the marching band all through football season."

"I thought you were a cheerleader?"

"I was, but only when I was little. My aunt gave me a baton when I was twelve. And the rest, as they say, is history."

"Twirling, huh?"

"I begged for lessons, and I got them for my Christmas and birthday gifts the next year."

"But the accident—"

"Ended my career dreams. Ha-ha."

I snickered, then caught myself. "I'm sorry." I looked at her again with a sympathetic pout.

"Thanks. So, my senior year was all books, all the time. I went to the prom, but that was it. I was depressed and so disappointed in myself for the stupid decision to get in that car and for missing out on what I'd hoped to be a glorious end to high school."

"But you healed up and went to college. Now you're successful, right?"

"I guess."

I'm not sure what was gained by that anemic pep talk, so I clammed up and focused on the road and traffic lights for a while. Silence filled the car, giving me time to enjoy the soft notes of her perfume. Oh, the joys of being around a beautiful woman. I'd forgotten too much about experiencing the feminine. Could I let Sylvie go? I wondered.

"I really appreciate this, you know. I suppose I could've figured out a way. Or bullied my boss."

I waved my hand. "Least I could do." There's nothing like an expression of gratitude to make me uncomfortable. Especially from Sylvie, who was in her current predicament because of my dog. I was sincere in saying that this is the very least I could do, but it also brought me an inexplicable pleasure that I couldn't resist. I didn't want to think about how spending time with this woman affected me.

I just wanted to get my book finished. Or I wanted John and Carol off my back. I love writing, don't get me wrong. The author's life is far less glamorous than advertised, though. It's a long slog. A truly lonely slog.

The loneliness hasn't bothered me so much as the arduous work of producing words. Writing is my calling;

I don't deny it. I have always enjoyed spinning yarns out of nothingness.

Since Evelyn left five years ago, that's all I've known. The calling. The long push. And, if I must admit it, I've allowed the loneliness to define me, as though my image as an author has special meaning when it's cloaked in solitude. That maudlin thinking was just too sad for words. I felt like a total loser.

I looked over at Sylvie. She stared out the window, cradling her wounded wrist in her right hand. The bumps on the road made her wince a little. I didn't like being the reason for her pain.

She sat up straight and pointed. "There. Can you fit?"

Without a word, I backed into a perfect space for my car. Sylvie grabbed the door handle.

"Whoa!" I put a hand on her upper arm. "How long will you be?"

She pursed her rose-lipsticked mouth. I couldn't tear my eyes away.

"Hour maybe."

"Great. Text me when you're about ready, and I'll swing by and let you know where to find the car. Okay?"

"Perfect. You're the best!" She slid out of the car so fast I didn't think I'd have a chance to wish her luck. But she spun around and bent over to look inside. "What're you gonna do now?"

I shrugged. I hadn't given it any thought. "Best of luck in there." I gave her a thumbs-up as she stood and pushed the car door shut. I inhaled her scent deeply and put the car in gear.

What to do, what to do? My fingers tapped the steering wheel while I drifted along city blocks, taking in the tall buildings around me.

Next thing I knew, I was near a chain hotel known for its Christmas decorations. I paid for a public parking spot and headed that way. The weather had changed to winter with a chilly vengeance. I hunched my shoulders to my ears and slid my hands into my jacket pockets. I'd have to run by my house to get some better winter gear if I didn't move back soon.

I stood mesmerized in front of an enormous Christmas tree. Yes, mesmerized. The tree itself was a glistening white, obviously artificial. Star-like white lights twinkled hypnotically. This was Christmas haute couture indeed. Metallic balls in fuchsia, teal, and lime green reflected the sparkling lights. What a modern feast for the eyes. I wondered if a child would like this tree or if its stylish gaudiness would lose place to the big green tree down the way, stuffed with fuzzy bears, beige owls, and black moose.

The glossy white-and-gray marble slabs on the floor led me past beautifully decorated shop windows and more trees. I enjoyed looking at this modern take on the holiday I loved, but I wished I'd gone by the old downtown hotel instead. Maybe I would later, as it deserved a less rushed visit to take in all the Christmas finery.

My phone buzzed in my jeans pocket. Assuming it was Sylvie, I pulled it straight to my ear and asked, "You ready?"

"Ready for what?" my mother asked.

Stupidly, I pulled the phone from my ear and looked at the phone screen. Yep, it was my mother. As if there were doubt.

"Mom! What's up?"

"I came by your rental, and you aren't here! I hear a dog barking."

Looking up to seek heavenly guidance, I laughed. "Mom, I got a dog."

"Really?" Her voice squeaked. She had let me have one dog as a kid, and when that went south—Barkley died, Pete was heartbroken—I never got another one.

I sighed. "You'll love Riley. Just wait."

"You're headed home now? I don't have much time."

"No, no. That's not what I meant." I chuckled. My mom's adorable and sweet, also a pragmatic, suffer-no-fool type of woman.

"So, where are you? Last time we talked, you were furiously writing. Deadline looming and all that."

"Helping a friend. I'll be back to writing by lunchtime." I sure hoped so.

"Who are you helping on a weekday—"

"Hey, Mom. I gotta run." I hated interrupting her, but I wasn't ready to explain Sylvie to my mom. She'd been nudging me for at least a year to "get out there." At forty, the last thing a guy needed was his mom offering dating advice. Talk about groan-worthy fodder for a bad book.

"Bye, dear! I can take a hint."

"*Ciao, bella*," I said in a syrupy voice.

Mom hooted as she hung up. She's always loved my ridiculous goodbyes. I started it with Mom in high school when I was also trying out my sexy talk for the girls, with marginal success.

Evelyn was never amused by it. How I missed the signs... Well, I needed therapy to figure out that relationship. I've never believed that my failed marriage deserved any posthumous investment, however.

My phone buzzed in my hand. Sylvie.

"Hey," I answered.

"I'm headed to the elevators now."

"Great. Um. I'm a few blocks away. I'll text you when I hit your corner. Stay inside, the wind's picked up."

"Thanks. See you soon."

She hung up before I could ask about her meeting. Well, we'd have car time for that. I looked at my watch and my stomach rumbled.

I found a spot and texted my location.

"Wanna get an early lunch before I take you home? I guess it would be brunch at this time of day, but is it brunch if it's on a weekday?"

"I guess. Yeah, I'm kinda hungry."

"Preferences?" I looked over at her as she fiddled with a strand of hair. She blew out a breath, and I could almost hear the wheels turning. Then she shrugged.

"You pick?"

Chapter 13

Sylvie

"When I was a kid, my favorite dinner was breakfast food."

A tiny smile softened Pete's mouth as he perused the plastic-encased menu. This was a wonderful memory, and I hoped he'd share more. Pete intrigued me, regardless of my hesitation about inviting him deeper into my world.

At the moment, he was the only "man in my life" as Angie called him every time we spoke. I swear she didn't care a minute about my broken wrist. Her curiosity about Pete overwhelmed every phone call.

Initially, she let my dismissal of Pete guide our discussions. I'd wave off the topic verbally and she'd back away a little. But her interest in Pete stayed on the back burner like a simmering pot. My second date with Tim fueled her chatter before and after it. Not a single Pete conversation for days! How glorious to not have to describe every text exchange or moment I'd spent with Pete. Angie's life must be more pitiful than mine if living vicariously through me brought her such glee. We're two peas in a pod: single working women too picky for our own good, I supposed.

After the second dinner, Tim texted me a few times. He made me giggle, and I welcomed the levity into my quiet existence. So far away from home, I'd forgotten many of the Birmingham connections we shared. They flooded into my brain and, suddenly, letting Tim into my life seemed like a grand idea. Why wouldn't I gravitate to the comfortable?

Reliving the car accident reminded me of Tim's devotion to me when I was hospitalized. I couldn't have asked for a better boyfriend. He forgave me for being with those crazy boys and he never seemed repulsed by my scars. Instead, he delivered constant sympathy and flowers. Granted, the daisies and roses were from his aunt's shop: the only way he afforded that weekly "flower shower" as Angie had called it.

Did it matter that I felt no spark when Tim kissed my cheek last week? It's a bit concerning. When we separated from the insignificant embrace, I studied Tim's face and I saw nothing I wanted. His boyish smile lit his face and crinkled his eyes. So handsome, yet even his looks didn't warm my heart.

Each time Pete's been around me, I couldn't help but compare the two men. Pete somehow won the contest, and I had no list of the winning requirements. It wasn't like I had a pro-and-cons comparison between them. The contest was emotional in its entirety—my checklist was fading the longer I remained in Pete's orbit.

The man had barely touched me, but my skin has sizzled whenever he got close. Don't make me describe what my body did when he studied me, which he'd done more than a few times. I didn't have the vocabulary for that level of heat and confusion. Just the mere mention of his mom's breakfast dinners created a warm flush that crept up my chest and onto my face. And I hated it, because it made me feel weak, like I'd lost all reason, and my logical side was losing a war with my heart.

Sticking with Tim would be yet another "settle" in my unfortunate relationship history. Andrew in Nashville was convenient—we worked together for a year until he left for another firm. A perfect time to move on, but did I? Of course not. Finding a new guy, figuring him out, was far too much work. So I kept hanging on to Andrew until I could conveniently ditch him for nobody in Richmond. Funny, huh?

"Having trouble deciding?"

"What?" I looked up from the menu and left my ruminations behind. Why was I thinking about anything else when I was with this amazing man? Because I shouldn't be torturing myself like that, that's why. I was going to get hurt.

"You've been staring at that like you're studying for a test." Pete smiled and aligned the edges of his menu with the table's corner. This movement drew my attention to the smudges on the high gloss shellac coating the table. I skimmed over one with my forefinger and realized the surface was clean.

"Um, I'm thinking pancakes. With bacon, of course."

"Excellent choice. Can't go wrong with the buckwheat pancakes here."

"All right then." I closed my menu and placed it on top of his just as the server showed up with pen and pad already poised. Sadie, so her nametag said, had spiky black hair and a pastel floral tattoo sleeve on her right arm. Her bright blue eyes sparkled. Pete gestured for me to order first.

After we made our choices and Sadie slipped glasses of water in front of us, Pete leaned back and leveled his gaze at me like I was hiding something.

"You haven't mentioned how your meeting went. Or is that info top secret?"

I snorted.

"Not good?"

"Sorry, yeah, it was fine. Not a secret. They signed as-is, so I don't have to do a rewrite and return for that. Thank goodness."

"Rewrites, ugh. I hate those too."

"Because the holiday is coming up, I won't have to chase them down again. I may not leave my apartment for the rest of the month. No meetings, yay!"

"That'd be good for your wrist, too. Less stress and movement." Pete unwrapped a straw and slid it into his water glass. I followed suit.

"So tell me about your favorite breakfast for dinner."

Then he spun an entertaining tale about his mother's Saturday tradition of making pancakes, eggs, and bacon. His dark eyes got a faraway look as he recalled the story. When he was ten, Pete found a waffle iron at a yard sale and paid two quarters for it. He loved the crispy edges of the waffles, and all the tiny square bowls designed to hold lots of thick syrup.

I couldn't finish my meal. The two pancakes were so large and oblong, they filled the cream-colored oval plate. The bacon came on its own little dish, which pleased me because I didn't want syrup on it. When I finished the bacon, I licked my finger and thumb. It was the best kind of crispy, just like Momma made.

Pete, on the other hand, cleaned his plate. He dabbed his mouth with the white paper napkin that he'd had on his lap. The man had manners. More kudos to Pete's mom.

"You ever go to church?"

I frowned at him. What kind of question was that?

"Um. Back in Alabama, yeah. I seldom attended church in Nashville."

"Would you like to go this Sunday? The choir's doing a cantata. They're fantastic."

"With you?" I asked stupidly. Who else would I go with?

"Me. And my mom. I pick her up since parking is so awful downtown. She hates parallel parking."

"Doesn't everyone?" I grinned at him. I was stalling while I came up with an excuse. However, meeting his mom would satisfy more of my ridiculous curiosity. She sounded like a cool lady, plus she'd raised Pete alone.

"I've gotten used to it while in this rental. The Fan is notorious for parking wars."

My brain seized on the word *rental*, but I didn't ask for details. Maybe I should go to church. It's Christmas season, after all. My favorite time of year, and the music always gives me goosebumps.

"What time and where?" I wrapped a bright pink scarf around my neck and slipped my good arm into my gray coat. I really needed to get home. My left wrist was begging for a pain reliever, which I had forgotten to put in my purse. Didn't think I'd be out for so long.

A dish crashed near the kitchen and both our heads swiveled to study the problem. Bright yellow egg yolk crept across the black-and-white checkered floor.

"Guess that's our cue." He grabbed the check and headed to the register.

"Hey, I should buy your lunch."

Pete waved me off as he pulled out a leather wallet.

The movement made me look at his jeans pocket, then down his legs, and up again. I liked what I saw. Oh dear. What was wrong with me?

"How'd you like that place?" he asked as he opened the car door for me.

"I'd go back again. And isn't that the true test?"

Behind the wheel, Pete continued the conversation. "My uncle Joe introduced me to The City Grill thirty years ago. Back then, the air was thick with cigarette smoke. I had to change my clothes when I returned home. Mom insisted on washing them separately, it was that disgusting."

"Do you still go with your uncle sometimes?"

"No. He passed away six years ago."

"Oh no, I'm sorry I asked."

"It's okay. Circle of life. I have pictures and memories. Fishing trips with him were the highlight of my days, well into my late twenties. Then I got too busy. Regrets, I've had a few, as the song goes."

"I understand. I guess he was your mom's brother?" I was making all kinds of assumptions about his parents. What do I know? Such an idiot. I gripped the edge of the seat with my good hand, a reminder to myself to quit talking.

"Yes, her older brother."

The car stopped. I unbuckled my seatbelt and opened the door.

"Eleven a.m., St. Peter's on Cary Street."

"Um—"

"Church on Sunday."

I laughed. "Funny me. I'll be there."

"Do you want me to swing by to get you?"

"No, that's okay. I'm going to try to drive on

Saturday. If it's a fail, I promise to let you know."

"Deal. Hey, wait. Saturday. Your Christmas tree. I wanna help."

I'd been thinking about not even putting it up, and I could not take any more of Pete's time. Or have him tease my senses all weekend.

"I may skip it this year. Thanks for the ride and the food. You've gone out of your way this week."

Pete waved me off. He seemed to be embarrassed by gratitude. But I dislike being dismissed, so I leaned back into the car.

"Listen, you really have been great to me since I broke my wrist. I don't know what I'd have done without you…um, your help. Sleep on that good thing. 'Kay?"

Pete's gaze stayed on me. His neck bobbed when he swallowed.

"Helping you is a pleasure." Then he put his hands on the steering wheel and looked away.

I smiled and closed the door. Sunday could be the last time I'd see him. I wondered how I was going to get through Christmas without my new friend.

Chapter 14

Pete

Maybe she didn't want to see me two days in a row this weekend. I was bummed out that Sylvie declined my help with her decorating. That rejection occupied my Thursday afternoon writing time, and I needed to kick my feelings to the curb and get more work done.

I didn't understand what had happened to change her mind about my offer. She hadn't acted as if she was pulling back. Quite the contrary, Sylvie had seemed to be really warming up to me. She didn't look away like she first had. Now she often held my gaze.

"Riley, ol' boy…" I patted the little guy on the head while I stared at my laptop. "Let's get outta here."

I grabbed my jacket and a baseball cap, headed for the front door. Riley, to his short-legged credit, beat me there. Maybe if he could reach the leash lying on the dark wood console table, he'd hold it between his teeth in anticipation. I can paint a picture, can I not?

The brisk wind had continued unabated since the morning. I stopped on the porch and zipped my jacket. I flipped up the collar for good measure, not that it would help.

Riley sniffed the air and turned left. I groaned but let him keep going the wrong direction anyway. Riley stared at the red-painted door of the mean dog we'd encountered a few days ago. Yesterday, we didn't walk this way. Finally, he decided to catch a scent on the sidewalk. He pulled on the leash until he had to take a nature break.

We finished circling the block within thirty minutes. I was frozen, so I made a cup of tea. I wrapped my hands around the mug to thaw my poor fingers. Riley got a treat, which he chewed slowly as if he were preserving the pleasure as long as possible. The wisdom of puppies.

That's why I wanted to help Sylvie with her tree. Spending time together would extend the pleasure I got from being around her. Soon, she wouldn't need me at all. I might still need her as a muse, but this wasn't about that. I wanted to decorate a tree by her side, watch her smile as her apartment became warmed by the holiday glow. I'd listen to her share Christmas stories while we put little green hooks on special ornaments.

"Dang it," I said to myself as I stalked to the dining room to find my phone.

I started typing furiously with both thumbs. I ran my hand across the top of my head, pondering the message I'd crafted. Did it sound like pleading?

I punched the back arrow. "If you have to ask, it is, Pete," I muttered, stopping halfway in the text. I re-read what was left before I hit send.

Nothing happened. No sign of Sylvie reading it or crafting a reply. I groaned loudly when I read my text again,

"Sylvie, are you sure I can't help you put up your tree? Seems like you could use some Christmas cheer. I'm at your disposal anytime on Saturday. Let me know."

Geez Louise, I sounded desperate, possibly a little too pushy. Stalker Pete strikes again! I'm a writer, for heaven's sake, and that's the best I could do? I kicked the leg of the dining room chair I used as my office seat. Riley's head jerked up and he growled.

"Ignore me, fella. Pete's having a bad day. A really awful, horrible day. Ya know why, Riley?"

Riley tilted his head—either contemplating an answer or agreeing something was wrong with me. Or maybe he was interested in what I had to say.

"Pete's an idiot, that's why." I refrained from kicking the chair again.

I looked at the time on my phone. Five. Perhaps she was cooking dinner? Out on a dinner date? No. She said the online thing hadn't worked out for her.

I wasn't hungry enough to cook, so I grabbed a bottle of beer and microwaved some popcorn. Riley plopped himself down on the carpet near my feet while I lounged on the couch. His motionless head was animated only by his brown eyes as they followed my hand, moving from the bowl to my mouth. *Sorry, fella, you're adorable, but no snacking for you.* I wasn't interested in cleaning up a mess when I woke up tomorrow morning because I'd fed him human food.

I had half an ear on the local news program. The rest of me was willing Sylvie to reply. I was a recent convert to a belief in telepathy. I'd left my phone near my laptop, hoping to reduce the teen-level angst that tortured every cell of my body. It didn't work.

Frustrated, I sat down in the dining room again. Chapter twenty of my current work-in-progress had been coming along nicely until today. I resolved to start the next chapter tonight. I flipped my phone face down and started writing.

The apartment grew dark around me while I focused on the words. Through sheer willpower, I got myself in the zone and wrote for hours.

I might have written well into the night, but Riley had other ideas. His whining brought me down to earth. I let him out the kitchen door and opened a second beer. I tipped back the brown bottle while I watched my new little friend sniff around the back yard. He'd really love the yard at the house.

Wait, what am I thinking? I glared at my reflection in the window glass. The night was as black as my mood had become again.

I wasn't thinking…these past few weeks were perfect evidence.

I checked my phone and saw the red notification and my heart went pitter-patter. Finding a message from a buddy, I clicked his name and called him, and then I thought about checking what time it was. It was actually a good hour to call a dad and husband, so I didn't hang up.

Max answered, "Pete! Where are you, invisible man?"

"I know, I know. Stuck in a book. Again. Miss hanging with my guys. I mean it."

A tiny dog bark crept into my awareness. Crud. Riley was still outside. Back to that question. What was I thinking? I let the poor guy in and gave him a doggie treat. Forgiveness was easy in this relationship, and he pattered over to his cushion, which remained in the hallway.

Max was talking about coaching his son's basketball team. I tuned in. We laughed about the stressors of our lives and promised to catch up after Christmas. I hoped we'd do what we promised. I couldn't remain an island, isolated from all the healthy stuff of relating with others.

Gotta take the good with the bad. Didn't know who said it, but I raised my beer bottle to the wise one and took the last swallow.

It was late, so I closed my laptop and switched off the few lamps I'd turned on earlier. Yawning, I checked my phone a final time and found that Sylvie had responded.

"That's fine. How about 10? I'll make coffee and have donuts."

I read the text at least five times. No subliminal message there, I decided. Was her response a little chilly? Hmm, I walked around the kitchen staring at it, contemplating the relative temperature of her feelings toward me.

I started to reply but realized I had nothing to say. I'd come up with something pithy in the morning, I figured. Thirty-six hours till I see Sylvie.

Who was that man in the mirror? I brushed my teeth and got ready for bed.

Playing it cool, I didn't respond to Sylvie's text until Friday afternoon. Pretty juvenile, I admit, but it's what I needed to do for my sanity.

"See you in the morning. Do you need me to bring anything?"

"All good here. Thanks."

Sheesh. I wanted to ask how she was feeling but had to play it like a grownup. Keep quiet, don't be a pest. I'd made that promise to her…when? Two weeks ago?

I ran a hand through my hair, scratching the top of my head.

"You're a goner, man."

Chapter 15

Sylvie

The next morning, Pete keyed himself into my building five minutes early. I answered the door with a mascara wand in my hand. Oops!

"Oh." I hid it behind my back.

Pete smiled and walked past me as I held open the door.

"Be right back."

When I returned, Pete was surveying the tree box and ornament bin. I'd moved them into the middle of the living room space and the bin had lost its lid. A tangle of green-wired lights draped over the edge.

"I know you want coffee," I said, hand on the pot's handle.

Pete startled a little, like he hadn't heard me return.

"Yes, please."

As I poured our mugs and set them on the island, I studied him, studying me. I'd chosen jeans and a creamy white knit sweater. The sleeves were full enough to cover my thick wrist splint without stretching. I'd wrestled my hair into a messy ponytail.

"You look more rested," he said it as a question, probably hoping I'd give a full update on how I was feeling. It'd only been a week, but bone breaks can heal fast when the person is healthy. Next week, the doctor would determine my wrist's status.

"I am feeling less tired. And this…" I held up my left arm. "Well, I'm not taking any pain meds."

"That's great."

We sipped our coffee, avoiding each other's gaze. I pushed a plate of donuts in his direction. He shook his head.

"Maybe later. Do you have a plan for your tree?" He pointed toward the box with his coffee mug.

"Um, yeah, kind of. I'd love to center it in front of that window. We'll have to move some plants. I already started moving a few that were on wheeled stands."

I pointed to a thick cluster of plants in a corner to the left of the floor-to-ceiling window. Pete studied the plant layout. I warmed to the feeling I got as I watched him think about things in my home.

"What if we move the taller plants over there? They'll still get light and not block the light to the others. I'll move them and we can see."

"Okay. Let me get a broom and dustpan. We'll find a mess, I'm sure."

After Pete dragged the plants left and right to create a wide-open spot, he swept up dead leaves and a few dust bunnies from the glossy cement floor. I think I blushed while I murmured in embarrassment over the uncleanliness.

"You should see my garage."

I gave him the tree stand. I worked hard not to laugh while he wrestled with the tree. Its hard metal branches swiped against his head until the trunk dropped with a clang into the stand. He grunted. Then I guided him through setting the three screws to make the tree perfectly straight. Pete mopped his face with a sleeve.

I clapped and whooped. It was hardly an

accomplishment, but Pete deserved the encouragement.

He ran his hands down the sides of his faded jeans and asked, "Okay, what's next?"

I held up a mess of lights, frowning at them. "I'm sorry I didn't treat these right during last year's take-down."

"No worries. You can learn a lot about a person by how they handle tangled Christmas lights, haven't you heard? I present you with a 'cool attitude.'" He bowed.

I helped find the ends of each strand, and soon we had five light sets ready to hang. They stretched neatly across the coated cement floor in skinny, uneven green stripes. This part of the decorating would also fall on Pete, who was getting a sweaty workout.

"Coffee break?" he asked when he wrapped the last light strand at the top of the tree.

"And a donut? You've got to be ready for one now." I swayed the plate in front of him like I was casting a spell.

Pete chuckled.

"Can I have the chocolate one?"

"Well…"

"Never mind, I'll take the caramel."

"Kidding. Take the chocolate! You deserve it."

"You're too kind." He winked at me as he took the chocolate one.

"Look who's talking."

"Did you try driving yet?"

"Early this morning, I went to the store. I did okay. It's just any twisting motion of this arm hurts. A little or a lot, it depends."

Pete nodded silently.

"Ornament time?"

"Yeah, now I can decorate! Exciting!"

Hanging the ornaments wasn't much of a challenge for me, thank goodness, although Pete had to hang the ones on the back of the tree, against the window.

"I want some of the shimmery ones back there. Then they can be seen from the street."

"All the way up here?"

"Yep, I'll have to show you. My window faces the side street."

Pete leaned forward to look down on the street. I started swaying to the Christmas song on the radio, "Merry Christmas, Darling"—a pretty song.

He smiled at me as I threw my arms out wide. "I love this song. So romantic. I've never been away from a true love around Christmas. Still…it makes me swoon."

"You're a romantic."

I made a face. "Maybe with the right person? I dunno. Maybe."

"No true love for you?"

"Not yet."

"A pig ornament?"

"Nashville barbecue."

"Ahh."

"I'd love a tree with ornaments from my travels. When I travel more, that is. One of these days, right?"

"Not to change the subject, but what's up with all these plants?"

"Okay, ready? It's a kinda long story."

"Fire away. I'm all ears." Pete said held his hands against the side of his head.

"Corny!"

And then I started my story.

"I love gardening, which I learned while kneeling in the dirt side by side with my Granny. She nurtured prize-winning roses, and she had a drawer full of blue and red ribbons, mostly blue ones, from the local county fair. I don't recall her being a braggart or overtly proud, but she framed the red ribbon she won at the 1999 Alabama State Fair for a tea rose she'd entered."

"She won a state fair ribbon? Wow."

"It was called Sunset Celebration. So gorgeous. My favorite from her garden."

"What color was it?"

"Like a peach-and-pink mix. No, wait a minute. I think Granny called it apricot, not peach."

"Okay, keep going. Sorry to interrupt."

"I don't have a garden, obviously, living in a city loft, but my balcony is green as all get out in the spring and summer. Gazing up from the street, you cannot miss this unit. It's the one framed by two lush ficus trees." I point out the gorgeous seven-foot-tall trees with dark glossy leaves.

"I also grow vines to twine through the railing. I buy those new each year. My floor to ceiling window catches the morning light for a few hours, and my plants are thriving in this place."

"I can certainly tell that. You've quite the green thumb."

"I reckon." I shrugged, kind of embarrassed by his rapt attention. To avoid looking at him, I ran the fingers of my good hand over a few plants.

"This schefflera and that Easter lily came with me from my college dorm room. I don't know how old they are in plant years, but they're pretty ancient."

"Plant years?"

"Well, you know…" I waved away the idea and brushed a loose strand of hair behind my ear.

"I *don't* know…but what's a guy supposed to do? Argue with a beautiful woman about plant ages? I've been known to debate the stats of my favorite running back, but not with a woman. That's reserved for the realm of buddies." Pete chuckled and came over to stand beside me.

I sat on the arm of my sofa and stared at the twinkling lights reflecting on the glass. My tree gave the space beauty in double-exposure.

"Your plants are impressive, Sylvie. You surprise me."

"Guess we should get the last of these ornaments hung, ya think? I'm sure you don't wanna be here all blessed day."

We both reached down into the last box and bumped heads.

"Oof," I groaned. I put my hand on my forehead.

Faces inches apart, his eyes dropped to my mouth. Then we were looking into each other's eyes, and I wanted to say something, but I was mute. He raised his hand just as I stepped away. Looking confused, he dropped it like he'd encountered fire.

"Are you okay? I'm so sorry."

"No worries. I'm okay. Obviously, as you've already seen, I've had worse run-ins." I held up my bangs to reveal my scars a second time.

With music the only sound in the room, we hung the last ornaments. I didn't feel confident about what was happening and wished I knew what to do or say. We had chemistry between us, but we weren't going to act on it. I avoided looking at him while we finished the decorating.

I may have been reticent about dating the last two years, but I had gotten out there. I wouldn't have met Pete otherwise. What was his hold-up? Was I right to be wondering about the signals he'd been sending? I already knew my signals weren't working right, considering my online dating fiascos.

Out of practice, I didn't know how to make the first move. I feared the rejection if I did.

"I think...I think we're done," I announced just after one o'clock.

"I like it. Hope you do."

The tree was covered in lights, ornaments, and a wooden-bead garland I'd made years ago as a childhood project.

"Thank you."

"My pleasure. I hope you'll excuse me to tend to the dog."

"Yup." I picked up his jacket from the back of the sofa. Wishing that he wasn't leaving, I had a sudden picture of us on my sofa. My head in his lap, and him looking down at me. I'd never stretched out on a sofa with a man like that, but I sure did want to experience it with Pete. Like the other evening, I was already missing him as he walked toward the front door. My eyes felt damp, so I blinked hard to stop my silly tears.

"See you tomorrow morning, right? Sure you don't want a ride?"

"I'll be there."

"Okay." He shoved his hands into his jacket pockets and strolled down the hall to the stairwell door.

When he turned to look back, I still stood there watching him.

Maybe he wondered what was going on in this silly head of mine.

Let him wonder. That'll make two of us.

Chapter 16

Pete

"She's here," I whispered into my mom's ear. She had the good sense to keep staring ahead, but she smiled and nodded. I didn't even have to say, "Don't look now," to my dear mom. She's spectacular, especially since she couldn't stop talking about meeting Sylvie and what a shocking development that I'd found a girl. At last! Her exact words.

Nothing I said in the car ride over convinced her that sharing a church pew with Sylvie was not a date. What had possessed me to invite her? Writing, maybe. Seeing her again would give me yet another fix, another vision of her, new words she'd spoken to replay in my head while I sat in front of my laptop.

I held up my hand to catch Sylvie's attention. She waved and started toward our church pew, which was about halfway down. I'd snagged a great spot, so Sylvie could see everything.

Sylvie had curled her dark blonde hair and kept her makeup light. Morning sunlight shone through a piece of blue glass and onto her shoulders. Her coat looked purple, like a queen's.

Mom and I slid over as she approached. We were in the middle of the church, along the center aisle. The sanctuary was about two-thirds full, better attendance than a summer Sunday. Not that I came every week.

Mom was a regular attendee, though.

"Don't you want to sit here?" Sylvie pointed to the spot at the end of the dark wood pew.

I shook my head. "You'll see everything better from there."

She slipped into the pew. Her left arm, thankfully, was against the pew end. The last thing I wanted to do was bump into her and make her grimace in pain. I'd done that a couple of times already.

"Sylvie, this is my mom, Anne Monroe. Mom, this is Sylvie." I leaned far back so they could greet each other.

"I wish I could say I've heard so much about you, but my son…" She shook her head and cast me a playful glare. I blew out a deep sigh.

"Here we go." I winked at Sylvie.

"Aww. You have a very polite son. Well done."

"Do you need help with your coat? I can help slip it off."

"Thanks." She leaned forward. I pulled the right sleeve off her arm and arranged the coat so it would cushion her back.

"Still not putting the left arm in, huh?"

"This coat's too heavy."

"I get it."

I glanced down at her outfit. She'd gone all out. She looked like a snow princess. Her knit dress was pale blue, with black trim along the shawl collar. Black tights and black ankle boots finished her lovely ensemble. She'd even worn pearl earrings and a necklace with pearls and shimmering crystals. She'd dressed to impress Mom. I liked that.

Mom and Sylvie chatted across me while I studied

this interesting young woman. She seemed to sparkle.

Mom would easily fall under Sylvie's spell. I didn't know what to think of it. Mom is not meddlesome, but she's always been clear that she wants me to be happy. And to her, happy means a woman in my life.

Though she'd spent her life single, she still believed that a man should not be alone. Mom might be itching for a grandchild, but she'd never applied any pressure. I'm grateful to her for that. And so many other things.

Then the organ music started.

Sylvie settled back against her coat. She pulled on it to resettle its bulk behind her, so I helped move it around. My hand brushed her shoulder. I don't know if she startled or if it was just me. I'd felt an electric charge.

Oh, boy. Focus on the music, Pete. Sylvie sang softly beside me.

I tried valiantly to keep up with Mom in singing the carols. She'd been a singer in high school. My three-year-old self went to church programs where Mom always had a solo part. I did not inherit any of her musical talent. Still, I am an artist of sorts, so I guess the apple didn't fall far from the tree.

She was nineteen when she had me, about to start her second semester of nursing school. She was a kid with a kid. I remembered times when we were barely making it. Somewhere, deep inside, Mom found a reservoir of patience for a rambunctious toddler boy and, later, a sarcastic teenager.

I've apologized a few times. Mom just giggles and waves me off with a, "You're such a good man."

If I have turned into a good man, Anne Monroe is the only reason for it.

After I butchered two Christmas carols, the choir

began its cantata program. Soloists and duets offered classical pieces—some familiar, some unknown. I settled into the pew, its hardness softening as the uplifting music flowed through me.

I occasionally watched Sylvie out of the corner of my eye. I heard her breath intake a few times. Her lips parted as she concentrated on certain songs. I enjoyed the musical presentation too and even more by observing her reactions. She clearly loved music, her fingers moving to the beat. I caught her wiping a tear during the last piece.

When the service was over, the three of us stood talking. A few parishioners lingered, mostly spouses and children of the choir members. A little girl in a red tartan dress peeked out at me from behind her father's khaki-clad legs. I waved my fingers and grinned stupidly at her.

Sylvie caught the gesture and turned to see the target of my antics. She smiled, then raised her eyebrows.

"Sylvie, how did you get here?"

"I walked," she said as I helped her into her coat. "Only about six blocks, I believe."

"Let me drive you home, though. It's too cold."

"Absolutely. Oh, good heavens…just come to lunch with us. It's a Christmas tradition." I couldn't believe Mom was inviting someone to our lunch outing. She can be possessive of her time with me, given our schedules.

"Oh, no, I can't intrude." Sylvie backed into the center aisle.

I watched these two women study each other. The murmur of other parishioners conversing about Christmas plans filled the silent standoff. That's what it appeared to be.

"It's not an intrusion. It's Christmas! Right, Pete?" Mom's expression told me everything: she was miffed that I hadn't jumped to support her invitation.

"Of course. I mean, yes, please join us."

"Well." Sylvie looked at her shoes. Then she looked at Mom and me and smiled. "I'd love to."

Chapter 17

Sylvie

I grew up going to First Baptist of Birmingham. All the right people attended that enormous white clapboard church. Momma constantly pushed my sister and me toward adults, to be introduced because you never know when you might need a job or a scholarship. One didn't dare miss church for fear of being the topic during someone's pot roast dinner.

I had failed to find a church during my first year in Richmond. I didn't search seriously, if I'm being honest. Safe from the prying eyes of my folks, I gave worship scant attention. I had looked online for Christmas events at nearby churches but had not decided on one yet. Breaking my arm had squashed some of my enthusiasm for holiday celebrations.

This Sunday was a little different. Being invited to church by Pete was a strange turn of events. The times we've eaten together have never felt like a date. The way he touched on topics and drifted off when it cut to the more personal made me wonder what was going on in that dark-haired head of his. Sometimes, he appeared to be on the cusp of drawing closer. In those moments, I welcomed the attention and the butterflies that fluttered around inside. Afterwards, I'd berate myself for encouraging any sort of connection with Pete. He's just all wrong. Right?

Hearing church bells and sensing a sweetness in the air that competed with the bright winter sky, I wandered the six blocks over to his small stone church. No denomination was noted on its sign or on the paper bulletin I picked up in the vestibule.

After the organ started, the congregation stood and spiritedly sang a carol I hadn't heard before.

Pete tried to sing the songs, but he lacked the enthusiasm of his mom. I figured he was like me, unwilling to sing out loud in public. What if I began a line before everyone else? I'd be exposed as tone-deaf.

I didn't really want to intrude on their Sunday lunch, but Anne Monroe was so likable. She was bubbly and warm, and her relationship with Pete was admirable. At least, what little I'd seen between them in church seemed comfortable, certainly easier than the relationship I had with my momma.

"Mom's an ED nurse," Pete said as he picked up a French fry.

"I guess you weren't working the night I took my nasty fall."

"I don't work nights, or at that hospital. I work across the river in the county."

"Oh. I don't think I've been out of the city limits here."

"How long have you been in Virginia? I assume you're not from here." Her warm brown eyes blinked at me.

"Alabama is my home. Accent's a total giveaway, I know. I've been in Richmond a year and a half." I took a sip of water, nervous that an interview was about to begin.

"You must miss home this time of year."

"I do, yes. I went home for all my first holidays here. This has been a weird year. I visited Alabama this summer. But some new clients kept me here for Thanksgiving. My Christmas plans are still up in the air, but I'm leaning toward flying home for a few days. My boss just demanded my presence in Nashville immediately after Christmas, so I won't get to see much of my family."

"Family time is so important during the holidays. Always, really. Pete here just loved Christmas with my parents. They made it so much fun for him. He didn't even mind coming home from college to see his Gigi and Paps."

"My grandparents made Christmas exciting for us, too. We used to pack up the car and spend the holiday at their house quite often. I always wondered how Santa found me."

"Christmas in Richmond is gorgeous. Have you gone out looking at the lights? Some of the houses are decorated to the hilt."

"No, I haven't. Last Christmas, I saw some pretty decorations, but I never just went out for a tour at night."

"When Pete was little—well, until he was about twelve—he begged me to take him around to look at homes. Then we'd go out for ice cream." She beamed at him, the memory causing her eyes to twinkle with joy.

Pete cleared his throat. We both looked at him like he was about to make an announcement.

"Sorry." He held up his hand. "Frog in my throat."

"Have some water, dear."

"I'll be right back." He pushed his chair away from the table, the legs making a loud scraping noise on the parquet floor.

As he walked across the restaurant, I watched a few people stop their conversations and gape at him. Though the man was tall and good-looking, the staring was kind of odd.

"Mrs. Monroe, thank you for inviting me. It's been a pleasure to get to know you."

"Call me Anne. It's nice to meet one of Pete's friends. Between his writing and travels, I seldom meet the people in his life."

"Well…I've only known him a short while."

"Right. His dog. I don't know what's gotten into him."

I couldn't resist laughing along with her.

"Riley's a sweet pup."

"I've got to manage that little doggie while my son goes to New York for a few days."

"Oh—"

"I'm back. What did I miss?" Pete slid into his heavy wooden chair and replaced the white napkin on his lap.

"You've got your mom watching Riley this week, I hear."

"Oh, yeah. Quick trip up to N-Y-C. Mom's gonna stay at my place."

I absorbed all this while Anne asked Pete some dog care questions. How long was Riley going to be left alone? I wondered.

"So, are you off work while Pete's gone?"

"Heavens, no, not this time of year. People get into so much trouble during the holidays."

"Um, Pete? How many days will you be gone? I hate to butt in, but do you think Riley will do well alone all day? Your mom's shifts are long. Right?"

"Twelve hours, mostly."

Pete ran a hand through his dark hair and scratched his crown. I'd started to look forward to that cute gesture. The man destroyed my focus, I swear.

"I leave Tuesday morning, back Thursday after lunch. Sheesh. You don't think I've thought this through, I take it."

I shook my head with a rueful smile.

"He can come stay with me."

"But he hurt you!" Anne exclaimed.

I picked up my knife and started cutting into a sourdough roll. I'd finished my salad but was still a little hungry.

"It's okay. Truly. I work from home."

"What if you stayed with him at my place?"

"Uh, I'm not really comfortable—"

"He likes my back yard."

I nodded. He was right about that. I had no yard, only city sidewalks.

"But your mom…"

Anne waved an arm across the table. "It's fine, fine, fine. Thank you, Sylvie, for putting the dog first."

She beamed at Pete as though he'd made a special discovery.

I wondered what had just happened. Out of a nice lunch, I had a dog-sitting job in a virtual stranger's house. Okay, Pete's not a stranger, but staying at his place seemed like a bridge too far.

What had I gotten myself into?

****

Angie was, of course, intrigued when I shared the details of my outing with the Monroe family.

"Oooh. He introduced you to his mother! That's some forward movement."

"Forward movement? Where in heaven do you get these phrases, Angie?" I swear my friend could drive me crazy and make me happy at the same moment.

"You gotta admit, Sylvie, this is progress."

"Progress?"

"Well, if you want Pete as a boyfriend, this is solid gold stuff!"

I snorted. Let's turn up the volume on the movie music. Angie probably sees me in a satin robe, prepping for some boxing event. A big fight to win my man. Geez Louise. I shook my head while I admired my Christmas tree. As Angie talked about how important it is when a guy invites you to meet the parents, I rearranged a few ornaments and adjusted the wooden bead garland.

"What're you thinkin'? I can hear the wheels turning hundreds of miles away."

"I'm listening and thinking about what all this means. It's just…"

"Sylvie—"

"Ang, stop. You'd have to see Pete in action. It's hard to believe he has relationship-building on his agenda."

"Well. Maybe you're holding back, too."

"Most likely."

Angie groaned. Some days, it seemed like my oldest friend was more invested in my love life than I was. I should probably tell her that, in hopes she'd back off. Instead, I bet she'd say, "Well, duh!"

Angie got off the phone to help her mom with Sunday dinner, and I was left to my own devices for the rest of the afternoon. I couldn't resist the urge to reflect on my dating problems.

Angie's dating advice has almost always been

useful, starting in middle school. Angie was the instigator who got me sneaking out of the house at age fourteen. Pinned in some wild senior's back seat with her and two guys, Angie had seen me at my best and worst. She was distraught after the accident since our injuries couldn't have been more different. She'd felt so responsible. That scary night drew us even closer, and she helped me get through my depression during our senior year.

Sure, it got harder once I moved out of state, but we've stuck together. I wish we saw each other more. I take on most of the responsibility for not hanging out with my bestie because I don't go home to Alabama as much as I should. Momma sure likes to remind me with her "last time you visited" commentary. I could avoid the guilt-tripping conversations if I behaved like Momma expected. Then again, I can use the whole adulting angle to establish grown-up boundaries with Momma, and that's going…well, just great. Sigh.

Angie has only ever worked in her family's gift shop, and getting away regularly has been next to impossible. For us to get together usually means I have to go home. And there are things about Birmingham I just don't miss anymore. Like watching my parents do their tension-filled dance around the silence—provoked by Daddy's wastefulness. I hate to say it, but the word *worthless* has flashed across my brain sometimes. A daughter shouldn't think like that about her own daddy. He's supposed to hold a dreamlike specialness in her heart. I know, so romantic—and unrealistic, given the man who fathered me.

My sister somehow missed the worst of the drama I had witnessed. A bit self-centered and four years older,

Constance Miller was gone more than she was home when things really started falling apart in our family. Her orbit around Daddy was tighter, and the gravitational pull between them powerful. It still remained so, at least from my vantage point.

As a young teen girl who craved a model relationship in her home, I was a spectator for all the what-not-to-do's in a marriage. Angie's parents were high school sweethearts who were still in love after having three daughters and spending decades together. I'm glad I saw what a perfectly happy family could look like. I'm no longer naïve enough to believe in perfect families, but I covet the rapport Angie has maintained with her dad. I reckoned that if her father had been like mine, she wouldn't be involved in the family business today. I knew one thing—that kind of forced family closeness I could not tolerate—not with my clan, anyway.

Then I witnessed another family bond—between a mother and her son. How hard it must have been for Anne Monroe to be a single mom. That such a pretty and sweet woman never got married was unusual, particularly for her generation.

My generation seemed less inclined to get hitched, but I've never imagined myself a spinster, though it's a worry of my dear mother. Because my sister married immediately after college, the same was expected of me. Momma believed we attended college to receive an M.R.S. degree, which is quite laughable. When I was a teen, Birmingham felt too small and old-fashioned, and I whined at Momma about "not livin' in the fifties anymore."

Chapter 18

Pete

Pleading for writing time, I didn't go inside Mom's house to see her decorations. I promised to come by after my New York trip.

But while sitting in her driveway, I dropped a text to Sylvie.

"You up for an adventure?"

Nothing. I closed my eyes and let the car's warmth envelope me for a minute. My phone, balanced on my jeans-clad thigh, didn't ping or vibrate, but I looked down at it anyway.

I threw my car into gear and backed out of Mom's driveway. I'd head Sylvie's way and hope she answered in the meantime. Mom and I had dropped her off about forty minutes before. Sylvie hadn't mentioned any plans for the afternoon, but I was still taking a chance.

I settled in to listen to the Christmas songs that had been playing since mid-November. You'd think my longtime penchant for listening to the local station that started playing carols during Thanksgiving week would spur me to decorate my place.

Living in temporary digs had forestalled any effort on that front this year. I'd been hoping against hope that my builder would put pedal to metal and get me back in my house in time for Christmas. Not sure I'd decorate, though. The big day was getting too close for any extreme efforts.

Sitting at a light, I peeked at my phone. Nothing. No thinking dots, either. Bummer.

What to do, what to do? I closed my eyes, questioning my motives and my irrational need to see her. Did I need to see her? My writing was going well. Okay, not at the moment. I laughed at myself and looked both ways before pulling forward—closer to Sylvie.

I kept heading her way, rationalizing that her place was on my way home.

After the next light changed to green, both my phone and the car's Bluetooth screen alerted me to a text from Sylvie. I hit the Listen button to play back her text.

"What kind of adventure?" A masculine British voice repeated her text.

"Christmas surprise."

"When?"

"Now?"

At another stoplight, I picked up my phone and saw the dots again. *Please say yes.*

"Will jeans be okay?"

"You'll be perfect. I'm five minutes out."

I grinned big, feeling much like a kid on Christmas morning.

Another text came through from Sylvie.

"K."

I wished she sounded more excited, but she didn't know how great this surprise was gonna be. I hoped she'd love it. Since I met Sylvie, I'd spent an inordinate amount of time hoping.

Unable to find a spot at her building's front door, I pulled onto the side street and texted her. I looked up, saw sparkling lights, and wondered if she was on the other side of that window.

"Around the corner on Lombardy."

"K."

I chuckled. These young'uns and their monosyllabic texts. Geez Louise.

I was tapping my steering wheel to "Holly Jolly Christmas" when Sylvie rounded the corner. The day had not warmed up, but she wasn't wearing a coat. She sported jeans, black knee-high boots, and a black sweater. The bright pink scarf she'd worn before snuggled around her neck and draped down the front.

She gave a little wave as she walked toward the car. I lifted my hand in return greeting.

"Long time, no see."

"Sorry. I should've come around to help."

She brushed off my apology with a shake of her head. "It's getting better. Day by day."

"That's good. I'd hate for a relapse, though, while you're watching Riley."

"Oh, I'll be fine. And so will Riley." She turned in her seat to look more directly at me. We were still sitting at the curb.

"I'm sorry for butting into your business with the dog. Especially in front of your mom. You must think I'm rude and overbearing."

"You overbearing? No. I'm grateful. I apparently had not thought this travel thing through."

I put the car in gear and pulled away.

"So…our adventure?"

"Patience, patience. You'll see soon enough. It's not far at all."

She settled back into her seat.

"Well, here goes then."

I parked the car on a side street near the old hotel we were about to visit.

"You don't mind walking a couple blocks, right?"

"Piece of cake."

She stepped out of the car while I held open the door. For a moment, we stood facing one another, close enough for our foggy breath to mingle. Then she dropped her eyes to the sidewalk. *Sylvie, what's that about?*

I pointed in the direction we needed to go. We walked in comfortable silence until we could see the hotel.

"Have you ever been to this hotel?"

"No, but I've heard of it. It's supposed to be amazing."

"Yes, it is. All year, it's a sight to behold, and the dining is very fine here. But Christmas is not to be missed."

I walked in behind her. Man, she had the perfect curves for jeans. Okay, I'm awful. And I'm a guy, so sue me.

Sylvie's intake of breath was audible. "Oh, my goodness!"

Her eyes twinkled with delight. She might have twirled around had she not been with me. I wondered how she'd describe this adventure to her friend Angie later.

"Can we go up those stairs?" She pointed to the center staircase that swept broadly at its base. Deep red-and-gold-patterned carpet beckoned. We walked right past a tree that nearly pierced the ceiling and up the stairs side by side, while I described some of the lobby's features.

"This is beyond amazing! My heavens, that's an

enormous gingerbread house."

Sylvie took off toward the ten-foot-tall structure. White frosting and copious amounts of candy decorated the house. Velvet ropes held back the curious and the hungry.

I studied her as she took it all in.

"I thought about this hotel the other day while I waited for your work appointment to end."

"You did?"

"I needed to pass the time, so I went to a chain hotel nearby. You should see those decorations, too. Much different. But I regretted not coming here instead."

She nodded and turned back toward the gingerbread house. Above its door, a sign read "Sweet Shoppe" in smooth white frosting.

"Did someone here at the hotel make it?"

I nodded at a sign on the wall. "Check out the ingredients. Fifty pounds of flour…"

"No way!" She came up beside me to read the sign, and the floral notes of her light perfume made me close my eyes for a second.

"Oh my gosh, I need pictures for Angie and Momma. They won't believe it."

While she took photos, I wandered over to look down at the lobby. The place was busy with guests milling about. Voices and laughter drifted up from the bar on the other side of the enormous Christmas tree. I heard a phone ring with a Christmas tune, and then Sylvie's voice.

"Hello. Momma? This is a surprise!"

After getting Sylvie's attention, I pointed to a red-velvet-upholstered settee against the railing. There I sat while she paced the landing and listened to her mother, who was doing most of the talking. She was engaged in a serious conversation, apparently. I tried to focus on the instrumental music floating through the hotel's lobby, but the anxiety in Sylvie's voice kept me listening to the soft, southern lilt of her voice.

"Should I come home now?" Sylvie turned to look at me and shook her head. She looked distressed. What on earth was her mother telling her?

"I'll wait to hear from you then. Thank you, Momma. Give Constance a hug from me. Okay? And I'll text or call her later."

I stood as Sylvie walked over. She crumpled against me; my arms flew around her. I felt her sobbing before I heard the cries. I wanted to know what the problem was, but I decided to just enjoy holding her. Well, not "enjoy" enjoy, you know. She was crying, and I cared about this troubling development, whatever it might be.

Her hair smelled nice too. After that embarrassing thought, she pulled away as if she'd read my mind. I hoped to heaven I didn't have a guilty look on my face. I felt like a thirteen-year-old boy.

"What?"

I did what I could to adjust my expression to a guiltless one. "What do you mean? What's going on at home? Can I help?"

"It's my sister. She…she…" Sylvie gestured with her right hand, like she was coaxing the words out, "she's pregnant. Finally. But she's on bedrest. Something's not going right." She leaned into me again. Her words were a mere mumble against my leather jacket. I stroked her back. Comforting words failed me.

"I'm so sorry, Sylvie."

Her nodding head rubbed against my chest. She may

have thanked me.

She took a shaky breath and ran her hands down her sides. "I'm okay. I just…"

I stood there. Silent, thinking. What was going on in her head?

"Are you going home?"

"No. There's nothing I can do. I know that. I've committed to you, remember?"

"It's okay if you want to head to Alabama. I can figure the Riley thing out."

Sylvie offered me a doubt-filled glance and walked over to the railing. We stood together, watching the people below us crossing the beautifully patterned carpet.

I watched anxiety pass across her face while she studied the hotel guests. Or maybe she was taking in the architecture and decor. The hotel was a lovely place. That's why I had wanted to show it to her. A lovely place to show a lovely woman.

"Hey, you okay?" I leaned in close, trying to get her to look into my eyes.

She shrugged and sniffled. I willed her to turn toward me. Then, I saw it.

"You have a…" When she looked up, I pointed at her cheek. She wiped at it, and I shook my head.

"It's right…here." She closed her eyes and let me touch her face.

"There." Smiling, I held up a lash on the tip of my forefinger. "My first eyelash. Ever."

I must've looked like a triumphant child to her.

She giggled. I liked that sound way too much. Her laughter was a velvety cream running over my weary and hardened heart. I swear her laugh had an Alabama tinge, warm with southern sunshine.

We stood there. So close. Both our gazes shifted to our mouths, and we leaned in. That I was about to feel those soft lips on mine made my brain go fuzzy. My heart jacked up.

Children squealed below. Spell broken, gosh darn it. We both looked down below.

Sylvie turned back to me. Her shy smile told me she'd felt something pass through us, too. Was she as disappointed as I was? That fleeting moment would reverberate in my brain for days.

"Can we go down and look at the lobby tree again? I didn't get any pictures before."

She was like a kid, and her enthusiasm was contagious. But, hey, I love Christmas. I even posed with her for a few selfies. I hoped she wasn't sending those off to Alabama. I didn't know how I felt about being the topic of conversation between Sylvie and her friend.

Why did that thought make me feel like the Grinch? I was just having a tough time working through this…this whatever it was. A relationship was not in the cards for me. Not now. But when? Was I happy all alone in that big house? At times, I was.

Five years alone had toughened up my edges, I hated to admit. Did I want things to change? Sometimes. But would I ever be ready? I'd believed so long that I couldn't change, and flashes of potentially permanent bachelorhood didn't sting all that badly.

Sylvie was something unexpected. And oh, the magic she'd brought to my writing.

"What're you thinking?"

"Want some hot chocolate? They have the best in town here."

"Really? Cool! Let's do it."

She tucked her arm in my offered elbow.

My prayer for a table in the lounge was answered.

"Tell me more about how your wrist is healing." She'd already mentioned it in the car, but I found myself at a loss for conversation. She seemed a bit more fragile after she'd heard her sister's news.

"I'm better able to manage my life, that's for sure."

"Glad to hear you're mending well, though." I wanted that moment at the top of the stairs. I studied her mouth, wishing.

"What a wonderful day! All Christmas, morning to night. Almost night, anyway. It's not dark yet, I think."

"I couldn't believe it when you told Mom that you hadn't seen much of our Richmond Christmas. You need to get out more."

"Work and more work." She dipped her spoon into her mug and lifted out a frothy glob of marshmallow. She closed her eyes and moaned softly.

"You deserved something special. I feel like I still owe you. And I'm glad you came to church and met my mom."

Sylvie surprised me then. She reached out with her good hand to touch mine resting on the table. The table's oil candle cast a flickering glow on the dark, glossy wood. We smiled silently in the darkness of the lounge.

The hotel must be the "place of broken spells" because at that moment, the server dropped the check on the table and scurried off.

We both reached for it, but I won.

"Gosh darn it, Pete."

"Let's go. There's something else you need to see."

"You have more to show me?"

"But we gotta run by my place to let out Riley. Then our Christmas lights viewing can continue. Okay with that?"

"No problem."

Slipping outside the hotel, we shivered in the cold. Sylvie looked up at the black sky. Her squeal made me jump.

"Snow!"

Sure enough, flurries drifted down upon us. A frosty sprinkle hit my cheek.

"Let's get going, then."

"This wasn't forecast, so it won't stick, will it?"

"It's Richmond. No telling, but most likely not."

"Oh well. I love snow, even though I never got to play in it as a kid. I could scroll through snow pictures online all day. So beautiful."

"Come on," I said, reaching for her hand. "More to see."

Sylvie yelped excitedly.

I would pay for having too much fun, not writing.

Chapter 19

Sylvie

Still on a two-day high after what I'd dubbed "Christmas Sunday," I wasn't prepared for the Pete I encountered at his apartment. Where did my charming Christmas guide go? On Sunday night after we got Riley relieved and fed, Pete drove us around The Fan for a light show.

By mutual agreement, we didn't sing along with the radio, but he'd turned up the radio volume. We could still hear each other but a festive feeling filled the car. Honestly, being in that tight space with him for hours melted my insides. If I hadn't been raised differently, I might have slid a hand down his thigh.

The snowflakes we'd seen outside the hotel were long gone, but they'd left a clean frosty scent in the air. On Hanover Street, he squeezed into a spot on the curb, and we got out to get a closer look at some of the houses and their decorated gardens. Pete definitely knew the best spots for Christmas cheer. The sidewalks were packed with families and couples out for an entertaining stroll. A few times, Pete's hand grazed my lower back and my muscles leaned against his touch. I wanted the evening to continue forever if it meant I'd feel the whisper of his fingers through my clothes.

When he dropped me off at my place, I was still wearing the jacket I'd borrowed from him.

"You can return it on Tuesday. No biggie."

Having his jacket at my place for two nights filled me with romantic notions of the man. I considered wearing it to bed, but wisely chose to leave it nearby. I slipped it on Monday morning until my scheduled video call. Pete's woodsy cologne taunted me from the threads of the ribbed collar. It was a delicious taunting, and I relished the teenager feelings of hopefulness.

On Tuesday, I arrived at Pete's with anticipation. We'd sip coffee and gaze at each other over the rims of our mugs. We'd share a memory of our Sunday together, and I'd thank him again for a lovely time.

But like a needle violently crossing a vinyl record, my hopes screeched to a noisy end in my head the minute he let me into his house.

"Here's the key." Pete handed me something. Just shiny silver metal sitting in the palm of my hand. No keyring, nothing. I stared at it, trance-like. I shook myself loose and got on with business.

"Oh, thanks. Any special instructions for Riley?"

"Not too many. I left you some general notes on the kitchen counter."

"Mind if I look before you leave, in case I have questions?"

I followed Pete while he scrolled on his cellphone. His jeans and red sweater looked nice. While admiring his broad shoulders, I matched his stride into the kitchen.

"Oh, and the guest room is on the left. Across from Riley's bathroom, ha-ha." He pointed toward the hallway. "Afraid you'll have to share my bathroom. I tried to clean it up for you."

Before I could respond, he was talking again.

"So, here's the schedule I've kinda had Riley on.

Obviously, you can switch it up if you have a meeting or whatever."

I stared at the yellow legal paper. His neatly printed notes harbored nothing complicated or surprising. My gaze drifted around the kitchen for the dog stuff. Pete discerned my thinking and opened a cabinet.

"Here are all of his food things and his favorite treats." Pete waved toward the open cabinet like Vanna White. I was proud of myself for not rolling my eyes. I wondered if he could recognize Riley's favorite anything. It had barely been a couple weeks, for heaven's sake.

"Cool. I'm sure we'll figure it out."

"I have no doubt that Sylvie, the dog whisperer, will figure it out." He fingered air quotes around "figure it out," so I gave him a kind smile.

Obviously, I had his phone number if I encountered any trouble. It was eight on Tuesday morning and I arrived early before I had to boot up my laptop and get to work. I hoped for some private time with Riley after Pete left, but he lingered like he wasn't ready to get out of the house. Or leave me alone in it.

"What time's your flight?" I asked. Maybe he just needed a kick in the pants.

He pulled back his sleeve to check his watch.

"I'm good. What other questions do you have? Oh, another thing. When you go out, Riley will pull to the left. Don't go that direction. Turn right and circle the block. There's a mean dog to avoid the other way."

His phone pinged, and he dropped his gaze. "Dang."

"What's up?"

"Stupid rideshare driver can't find me. I'll miss my plane."

"Oh, dear."

He headed toward the front door. I hadn't noticed his gray hard-sided suitcase sitting in the front hall. He lifted his leather jacket off a coat hook and slipped into it.

"I'm not the best traveler, I must admit. No patience."

I nodded. No response seemed necessary.

"Riley itching for a walk?" I wiggled my eyebrows at the dog, who sat at our feet watching the dog-sitter orientation.

"Huh. Maybe he's anxious to get you all to himself." Pete wiggled his eyebrows at the dog, too. He'd directed way more affection and warmth toward the dog than the dog-sitter. Wait a minute, was I craving affection from this man? I mean, well…I dunno what I want these days. Pete checked most of my boxes. Let's be real—he'd probably check the dating boxes of every normal woman. Yet I still found him lacking. *Confused* didn't begin to explain what was going on in my head and heart.

I missed the warmth of our Sunday adventure. He'd held my hand! And when he opened the door for me, I paused and looked in his eyes, willing him to kiss me. My signal machine failed again, but we had a wonderful time riding around the city looking at lights. Riley had sat on my lap, occasionally licking my hand. Pete doubted the wisdom of inviting the puppy along, but I'd convinced him to give Riley a chance.

I woke up excited about seeing Pete. But after the fifteen-minute orientation, I just wanted him to leave.

A gray sedan pulled up. He gave the dog a final pet and me a polite salute. Geez Louise. And when I heard a car door shut, I let out the breath I'd been holding.

Riley and I had some catching up to do.
****

With Pete finally gone, I hooked the leash to Riley's collar and opened the front door. He bounded down the three front steps. "Bounded" being a slight exaggeration given his skinny, five-inch legs.

Despite Pete's warning, I allowed Riley to lead me to the left. "Let's go meet this mean old dog, buddy." He looked up at me and jauntily walked in the prohibited direction.

We'd completed half the block when a vicious bark jerked our attention to a red brick house. Growling began in earnest. Riley was the growler. Geez Louise. I should've listened.

Riley tugged toward the iron gate protecting us from the nasty dog on the other side. Then I had to laugh. We were staring at a Chihuahua—his or her snarling sharp teeth bared for all the world to see. The tiny dog wildly snapped at us from behind the storm door's glass.

Riley snarled and pulled at his leash. Wrangling him was like...I dunno. Never been to a rodeo, but maybe like that. All I knew was my right shoulder hurt from him pulling against me. My left wrist ached from the effort my body put into the fight. This was a battle of wills I was determined to win.

A woman came to shut the wooden door. She looked at us as though we'd started it all. Her bright lipstick twisted in a mean sneer. Dog and mistress, hmm.

Did I clang a stick on her iron fence? No! Her dog was on high alert, probably all day long. I wasn't taking the blame for her dog's reaction. Even though I'd been warned. Now, that...that was on me. Pete had ticked me off, and I'd chosen to ignore his warning.

Why did I let him get to me?

Unable to pull my coat belt tighter against the chill, I decided to head back. I tugged on Riley's leash a final time and did a U-turn on the sidewalk. We didn't need any more drama in our first hours of dog-sitting bliss. Riley made a pit stop beside a tree on the street side of the sidewalk. Thank goodness squares of dirt and skinny trees dotted the sidewalks along this street. The Fan was a beautiful place to walk around at Christmas too.

I determined we'd take regular walks over the next two days. Christmas had gotten into my heart on Sunday when I was with Pete. I hadn't gotten any work done yesterday except for a call with Patrick. I had fiddled with my tree, lit a few Christmasy candles, and stared out the window. Every hour, I checked my phone for messages from him, though I knew he'd be getting ready for his trip. I wished the time with Pete had lasted a little longer, that's all.

I thought he'd felt an extra dose of Christmas spirit too. How had the feeling washed off him so soon?

Riley started pulling back toward the mean dog's house. I needed to get to work. Patrick and I chatted at nine almost every morning.

Stupidly, I'd left the front door unlocked. The silver key had been bobbing in my right coat pocket since Pete handed it to me.

I was fishing a doggie treat out of a box when my phone rang. Shoot! It was Patrick already. The oven clock said it was almost nine. I gave Riley a little pat and answered the call. While Patrick asked me about my weekend, I settled at the kitchen counter with my laptop.

One exhausting hour later, Patrick let me get back to my reports. The university's holiday break meant I didn't have my intern to pull the data I needed. Lunchtime came and went.

A whining at my feet reminded me I had a job to do. What a wonderful dog Riley was, though! He'd slept and lounged for hours while my work intensity had made me forget about him.

"Oh hey, boy. Let's go outside. Yeah."

Opening the back door, I followed him into the yard. While Riley sniffed around and tinkled on a shrub, I looked around the property. Not much to see. A wooden fence on all sides and a little red shed in the back right corner. Riley trotted past me and jumped up the two steps into the kitchen. Good boy.

I unpacked the bag of food I'd left on the counter this morning. I wasn't hungry, so I went on an exploration of the apartment.

My phone rang the minute I got to Pete's bedroom.

"Hey, Angie. What's up?"

"Girl, you're a hoot. What's up? LOL. What's up at Pete's apartment is the real question."

I rolled my eyes, instantly sorry I'd told Angie about this little adventure when we chatted last night. I should have known she'd call me for a big scoop.

"Hang on. I need to check something."

I scooted silently through the space. My gaze swept each room from floor to ceiling for cameras or other electronic devices. God forbid Pete accused me of searching his apartment when he got home.

"Okay. We can talk."

"What the heck were you doing?"

I slipped outside to the back porch and whispered, "I was searching for recording devices."

"Oh, for pity's sake, friend! He's making you stay

at his place. Who's not gonna look around?"

"True. I kinda sensed some weirdness when I arrived this morning."

"Weird, how?"

I thought carefully about my words. I took too long, so Angie piped in.

"Well? Possibly he was just as uncomfortable with you being there. Right?"

"No, he was a bit frosty."

"No kisses goodbye, huh?" She's my best friend, so she knows how to push my buttons. After twenty years of friendship, I should be permanently sore from having my buttons pushed.

"Just so you know, I am rolling my eyes right now!"

"What about pre-travel jitters?"

"Um…what?"

"Well, like he doesn't enjoy flying or something."

"Never mind my complaint. You might be right. His ride was late."

I heard the rustle of paper and whispers on Angie's end, so I knew she was at work.

"Hey, is this not a good time?"

"Who called who? Things are not too busy here yet, so I'll go to my office so we can chat more."

"I guess you've had a strong Christmas?"

"Oh lawd, yes. It's been fantastic! I may get to take a vaaaayyyy-cay next year. A real honest-to-goodness vacation. Where should we go?"

I rolled my eyes again. I shrugged before I remembered she couldn't see me.

"Listen. This Pete thing. I have a powerful feeling he'll be gone from my life before the year's out. We have no future that I can see."

"You like him, though?"

"I've enjoyed the times we've hung out, sure."

"Not an answer."

"Are you in law school now?"

"Hardy-har-har. You're so funny."

"Angie, you know me. Too well, I might add. He just doesn't check all the boxes."

"You and your dang boxes. Timmy Jones ticked all the boxes and you're avoiding him!"

"What if I'm a commitment-phobe?"

"Hilarious. You're picky, and that's okay."

"Is it, though? What if a perfect man gets away because I'm stubborn?"

"When you know, you know. Same goes for me."

"Have you been out on any dates lately? I'm sorry I forgot to ask."

Angie had taken a page from my book and started a dating profile on Flirtable. I'd heard about only one date so far.

"Nah. The store's too busy. I'll pick it back up in the new year. The one and only date I had offered to take me to a concert he had tickets for last weekend. I already had a thing to go to. Story of my life. Bad timing, and worse timing."

"All in good time, I suppose. Our biological clocks aren't ticking yet. Well, not according to the women's magazines."

"Change of subject. How's the apartment tour going? Find anything juicy?"

I'd been watching cars go by through the living room window while we talked.

"Snooping forgotten! Hold on, let's try the bedroom. Best place to sneak around, right?"

"You know it, guuuurrrrlllll!"

I pulled open the first dresser drawer. The brass handle clinked back onto its backplate.

"Oh goodie, dresser drawers, right?"

"Yep. And…they're empty except for one with a couple of T-shirts I've seen him wear under his plaid flannels. Thank goodness there's no underwear."

"Try the nightstand."

If Angie had been there, she'd have wiggled her eyebrows suggestively.

"There are two. I'm going in!"

She quit laughing when I reported there was nothing to see.

"Sheesh. What's with this guy?"

"No idea. I guess I haven't been curious enough to ask him lots of personal questions. It's like he holds me at arm's length most of the time."

"Hmm. Well, trust your instincts, I guess. But…"

"Closet's a bust. One shirt hanging here. But what?"

"It's just…well…"

"Spill it, Ang. I can take it."

"Can you, though? Can you really handle the truth, my dear friend?"

Angie's question reached across the miles, pinching my heart. I stayed silent as I walked back to my laptop in the kitchen.

"Well…I…it just has seemed to me…um…"

"Oh my heavens, Angie! Spill. It. Are we friends or not?"

"You're in love with him. There, I said it. Satisfied?"

Angie had said it and I had heard it loud and clear. I'd made a mess of it. What had I done?

"What you've done, my friend…"

I laid my head on the cold kitchen counter. I had asked that question out loud. Goodness gracious. Angie's voice cut through my boiling emotions.

"…is fallen in love with an apparently great guy. Maybe you just can't see the wonderful right now. Have you misjudged him? Seems like you need a little more information about him before you toss him off a bridge. I'm not judging you, girlfriend. You do you. I'm here for you. No matter what."

That was quite a speech by Angie. From hundreds of miles away, she saw things I was too stubborn or blind to see. I could count on her, whether I chose Pete, if he wanted me, or I moved on with my life.

"I'll figure it out, right? Don't I always?" Of the two of us, I liked to believe I was the most practical one. Not that my logical mind had served me well in the romance department all these years.

"Hey, I hate to do this, but Nessie is waving at me. A truck's here. It's probably a Valentine's shipment. Crazy, right?"

"Valentine's Day is the last thing I want to think about."

"Kiddo? You'll be okay."

"Yeah. But I might end up with a broken heart for Christmas. The question is…will I break it, or will he?"

Tears threatened. Gosh, it was all too much. What the heck was I doing at his place?

Chapter 20

Pete

Glass and stone sailed past the taxi as I got closer to my publisher's offices. Leaning against the cold window, I stared up at the pale winter sky. It had a soft blue cast even though the cab driver reported snow was in the forecast. Snow is pretty…in Virginia, not in this city.

I didn't have the time or patience for a messy city snow. The one I remembered was ten years before, when I lived here. My memories of it were vivid: blaring car horns, the swoosh of slushy water hitting my pants legs, wet, frigid air. Sounds awful, right?

I was living back in Virginia five years later. By then, confidence—or some shade of arrogance—made me brave enough to try an existence hundreds of miles from my agent and publisher. I had the bull by the horns, so I thought.

I nearly wasted my first year away from Carol's eagle eyes. She almost fired me. Fresh off my third successful novel, I thought I could manage both my work life and my personal life. But back at home, I found distraction with family and friends. I hadn't realized how much I missed seeing the people who knew my heart. No one in New York saw my heart, except maybe Evelyn. No wait, not true. Too often, she'd looked right through me as if I didn't exist.

We'd been married four years when Evelyn came to Virginia with me, but she treated it like a game. She picked at everything I loved. Richmond was so provincial to her, so slow and backward. I seldom responded to her complaints because I took them as personal affronts. That's on me, I admit. Growing up there, I was in love with the place—the sights, sounds, and smells. And history embedded everywhere. What an amazing place to grow up. Then the rest of Virginia—all of it exceptional.

If I ever quit writing, I can work for the tourism board. I should have focused back then on the merits of our lifestyle and defended my hometown.

Slowly, Evelyn pulled me away from friends until I could barely squeeze in one football or basketball game a season. A creature of the bustling city, my wife endured the annoying gentility of Richmond for over two years. Endured was her word. Gosh, she was miserable. She made me suffer even more for making her move away from the things she loved.

She got plenty of city fixes when she flew back to New York for meetings at her literary agency. Thank goodness she wasn't my agent, though she worked at the agency that represents me. And she is still there, with an office across the hall from my agent, John. She's a tough lady, and she was talented enough to wrangle a deal to work long distance so she could stay married to me. I showed my gratitude regularly.

I had been desperate to get out of New York, and I wanted to make our marriage work. In retrospect, I was far more interested in living in Virginia than in keeping Evelyn around. I have oversimplified that dynamic. I blamed her as things disintegrated, but I saw there was fault enough to go around. It wasn't a fifty-fifty split of blame, either. Moving out of New York was a signal to Evelyn that I didn't think she was enough. Or so she told me, in so many words.

She was dating a lot, so I heard. Trying to find another "big fish" was how John put it. John's always been on my side, if one can find any good side to be on around an imploding relationship. Debris contaminates everyone, and John didn't come out unscathed. He'd become a good friend, my only friend in New York, when I was putting up with all the big city garbage I hated.

Whenever I see her at the agency, bitterness is like a cloak around her. John and I had discussed whether Evelyn would be around during my visit. Apparently not. I was relieved that I wouldn't have to say a quick "Merry Christmas" at her door, then skitter off like a shy teenager. Avoiding interactions with her suited me, even though she was generally civil.

Before she left me, John told me about Ted Reynolds, a new writer he'd represented until Evelyn got her talons in him. I didn't appreciate how she treated my editor and friend, but the entire story made me suspicious. It was never in me to accuse her of cheating. With our marriage clearly approaching its expiration date, lobbing such accusations wouldn't have helped me any.

She ended it in her usual businesslike fashion. There she had stood in our luxurious bedroom suite, a perfectly manicured hand on the top of her red hard-sided suitcase.

"I'm not coming back. I've come to realize just how much happier I am when I'm in New York."

No recriminations about wishing things were better,

or how much she'd really tried. She hadn't.

I'd stuck my hands in my jeans pockets and nodded. I pursed my lips, perhaps thinking of a plea to keep her, but nothing came.

Instead, I said, "I'm happier when you're in New York, too." I turned on my heel and walked down the hall to my office. The morning sun was sparkling on the just-cleaned picture window, and strangely, it had made me smile.

Evelyn wasn't the door-slamming type, but she closed the front door firmly enough for me to know she was leaving. When I told her I was happiest when she was away, her face nearly crumpled. She must have expected me to beg her to stay and work things out. I might have if my head hadn't been so embedded in the sixth novel of my series. And that's more reason for not dating much since Evelyn left five years ago. I'm a workaholic and not desirable company.

I'd hurt her with her own words, but she never viewed it that way. What I saw clearly at that moment was how one-sided everything had been during our last two years together. And I'd allowed it. Feeling guilty about taking Evelyn out of her element, I had let her do things her way. Blame was still all I could muster when I thought of the end of our six-year union.

When she walked out, I vowed never to be such a fool again.

The cab driver brought me out of my sad ruminations. "Here ya go, mate." His Aussie accent made me wish I'd talked to him instead of drifting into my dark memories.

I scrambled with my wallet to get him some cash, giving him too much just so I could make the quickest escape possible. I grabbed my suitcase and flew out the back door of the taxi. A blaring horn made me jump, but when I looked over my shoulder, I learned it wasn't meant for me. My cab was long gone.

Fast. That city life was too fast for me. I looked up at the beige stone building and set my shoulders. John was meeting me here at Carol's office. I didn't think it was a call to the principal, but I was nervous anyway. Dropping everything and flying somewhere at the last minute was enough to make even a successful adult have qualms.

The executive suite was decked out for Christmas. It reminded me of the glitzy tree I'd just seen at the modern hotel at home. A silver metallic tree, gold and silver garlands, and red poinsettias added to a festive air. John sat on a white leather bench outside Carol's office. The French doors leading into her suite were closed.

He stood and shook my hand. He'd dressed up— gray suit, white shirt, blue tie. My agent was taking this some kind of serious.

"So what's the deal, man?"

"Dunno, Pete. Kinda cloak-and-dagger sounding stuff from Carol when she called me."

The doors opened and Carol, dressed in royal blue, greeted us with arms open wide. Not for hugging, just a broad gesture of welcome. Carol didn't hug. At least, not her clients.

"Gentlemen! Come in, come in. Let's chat over here." She motioned to a seating area that was glass and chrome, encircled by more white leather upholstery.

"So, a mystery, Carol?"

"All in good time, John. Pete, tell me about your current work-in-progress. Where are we on that?"

The royal "we" that all great publishers are inclined to employ. I sighed.

"Progress has been good. How are the pages you've seen so far?"

"Fine. Your editor, Beau, won't start on it until we have all pages. What's your finish date?"

She's constantly all business, but this felt particularly pointed.

"Carol, are you disappointed in my recent work? I mean, I can't help but—"

She held up a slim-fingered hand. Her wedding band and diamonds glinted in the frosted sunlight coming through the corner windows.

"You're fine, Pete. More than fine, actually. Rather than delaying our main conversation, let me call in Jim Riser. We can get on with it." Carol got up and buzzed her assistant.

Jim Riser? Why did that name sound familiar?

A tall fellow in a navy pinstriped suit followed her into the office. His fading blond hair was cut short. I detected a little silver in his cropped beard.

We all shook hands while Carol made the introductions.

"So, John, this is a little out of the ordinary. Jim approached me, rather than your agency, about gaining film rights to one of Pete's books. I kept it under wraps as a Christmas surprise!" Carol clapped her hands together, beaming like a proud mother.

"Film rights?" I asked.

"Which novel?" John stood and began pacing behind my chair. I stifled a smile.

"The first one! Isn't that exciting? Who could've imagined that *The Gentle Killer* would get a nod from

Hollywood!"

It all played out in slow motion. A movie deal?

I thought I was dreaming, but then Jim coughed. "Carol and I go way back. Sorry I didn't come to you, John. Obviously, we have much to work out. Screenwriting, contracts—"

"Sure, sure," I interrupted. This was heady stuff, and I needed a moment. More than one. "I'd like to talk this through with my agent first, though."

John nodded thanks in my direction. He looked as floored by this news as I was. Naturally, he had contractual concerns since the deal should've gone through his agency. Every agency has a special division with agents who handle all non-print rights, called subsidiary rights.

"Shall we meet here again tomorrow, same time then?" Carol stood beside Jim.

John and I nodded in unison.

"Good. Come back at two."

I didn't feel dismissed, but the meeting had quickly taken a frosty turn. My publisher must have expected corks popping instead of questions and legal concerns.

John and I caught a cab back to his office, and he talked the entire way while I drifted into a thick fog. I'm an author of books, nothing else. Making movies and all the accompanying issues weren't in my wheelhouse, and I was certain I didn't need another complication in my writing life.

The agency ordered sandwiches and drinks. We hunkered down with the legal staff and talked well into the night. I learned far more than I've ever wanted to about movie-making and stupefying contractual language.

At some point during the meeting, I checked my phone, but all was quiet. I thought about Sylvie and Riley. She hadn't called or texted, so everything was okay there. The urge to call her with this news overwhelmed me. This was worth sharing, and I wanted to tell her before I told anyone else, including my mom. There was one minor—no, make that major—problem: she knew little of my real life. I'd offered no details about the apartment or my work. I can't explain why I'd kept it all under wraps, but I suffer from not wanting to be known. Cute for a famous writer, right?

Because if Sylvie didn't know me, I could keep myself at a distance. Then I'd never get trapped by some unwanted emotional involvement.

But I was beginning to see how stupid I'd been to shut myself off from that incredible woman who had magically appeared in my world. I knew one thing for certain: my approach to life was absolutely no fun anymore.

What was I gonna do about it?

Chapter 21

Sylvie

I stood in front of Pete's door, staring at the peeling brown paint. He didn't respond to my repeated knocks, so I stepped over to peek through the dining room window. At that moment, the front door opened. Pete's voice carried into the spot I'd just vacated.

I returned upright in front of him to find he was on the phone. Another man was speaking loudly, or Pete had him on speaker-phone. I waved with a big smile. Then I pointed to the small Christmas tree on the porch beside me, mime-like. The only thing I was missing was the beret and black-and-white outfit.

Pete looked down at the little tree, then back up at me. He gave me a thumbs-up and turned back into his house. I was supposed to follow, I guessed. And carry the tree by myself. I rolled my eyes.

I have found Pete to be a very distracted man. Don't get me wrong. He's attentive, too. But he gets a faraway look in his eye sometimes, like he's telling himself a story. Guess if I were always looking for work, I'd be stressed out and digging for any kind of writing project I could find.

Yes, that could sound like a complaint, but I had been extremely busy when I met Pete. Then my broken wrist set my work projects back a few days until I could settle into a new way of maneuvering my bad hand around the laptop and my car. My clients were incredible in their understanding. Probably a bit of Christmas spirit going around. And I have a lovely smile, if I may say so myself. And Pete's said so too, so there's that.

He did so much for me over the weeks my left arm was out of commission—I had to do this special thing when I discovered he had no tree. Who skips that? And his mom said he loved Christmas! Complete nonsense, I thought. He helped me with mine, so I wanted to make things even.

While dog-sitting, I decided to surprise Pete with a tree, but in that moment, I questioned my decision. It was only two days before Christmas. This was just a silly idea, embarrassing even. Emotional things always make my insides tie up in knots. And my hands get all sweaty. One time in middle school, I had to give a campaign speech in front of the entire seventh grade. I'd chosen that particular torture, but still my stomach clenched so hard that I stooped over during my speech. And my note cards, well…they were damp and wavy along their edges.

I wouldn't deny I liked Pete. Angie had been riding me about giving in to this emotional roller coaster. She was willing to come up here and date him herself, so she said. I'd fed her silly obsession with too much information. But there was "the problem" I couldn't handle. It was unacceptable to me that things didn't seem stable around Pete. Other than his doting mother, that is. She was adorable and I would love her as a mother. Pete was a lucky guy. I love my momma, don't get me wrong. She's amazing too, just in different ways.

But the Pete thing. I didn't know what to do about my feelings for him. Half of me wanted to run into his arms and the other half was in flight mode. When would I ever let love have the upper hand?

Love? I sighed, but Pete didn't even turn around.

As his back retreated, I shrugged, grabbed the tree by its tip, and dragged it in. Needles fell like breadcrumbs. I didn't need any help getting it out of my trunk, then up his short sidewalk. I'd gotten lucky with parking. Most guys would have grabbed it, though, especially since I still had a bandage on my broken wrist. But he was on the phone. It's Sunday, so it couldn't be work-related, I thought.

As I entered his living room, I glanced at the corner I thought would be the best place for the tree. A speaker sat there, but I could move it. Did it matter where I put the tree? This place was so devoid of personality, one wondered who lived here. Pete's book piles leaned in every direction, so many books I didn't give them much of a glance. But I'd spent too little time there to know anything about the owner.

I dashed out to my car to get the tree stand I'd found at a flea market. The bin of ornaments I hadn't used this year sat in the front seat. But I couldn't carry everything in one trip.

Returning inside, I caught a bit of Pete speaking.

"Listen, John, I appreciate the pep talk. It's coming along fine now—"

The voice on speaker said, "Don't let Christmas get in the way."

"Yes, yes, I know about Christmas. But I have a schedule I'm keeping, so the pace will continue."

"Don't let us down."

Pete laughed.

"Right. Like I've ever done that to you and Carol.

John, I gotta go. Sylvie just arrived."

"Sylvie? The reason you're writing again! What a stroke of luck that you've managed to keep your muse around."

Pete turned around, smiling at his phone.

I stopped just inside the living room. The tree stand fell to the floor.

Muse?

The rush of my pounding heart filled my ears, like I was standing under a waterfall. My face felt frozen. I couldn't blink.

"Gotta run, John."

Chatter came from the speaker until he shoved it in his jeans pocket.

"Sylvie." His eyes flitted over my frowning face.

"What do you need a muse for?" The question tumbled through the tears clogging my throat. I couldn't swallow.

Pete rubbed the hair on the crown of his head, his face scrunched in thought. Or maybe it was anguish.

Not sure. Didn't care. Okay, yeah, I cared, but I didn't want to. I suddenly had too much information about things that were distressingly unclear. Thoughts ping-ponged around my head, but nothing stuck.

"Sylvie, I can explain."

"Awful stories start with those words. I heard them all my life at home."

"No, no. This is a good story. A fantastic story."

"That part where you 'managed to keep me around'?" I made air quotes with my hands. My left wrist sent a needle of pain into my forearm. I winced.

"Hey, wait. You're hurting. Come here and sit with me. That's not what John meant."

"I don't think I should stay." The polite Southern Sylvie visited my brain. The sassy version would have stomped out after she yelled something mean. I rarely invited Sassy Sylvie anywhere, because she'd embarrass me. And Momma would be furious.

"Please." His voice ticked higher into a pleading tone.

A tear trickled down beside my nose. Where'd that come from?

It literally made no sense for me to be that way, but I'm such a sucker for a penitent man. I should not be. I'd witnessed one in front of my mother every week during my last few years at home. That alone should've made me run screaming out the front door and put the gas pedal to the floor. But just call me codependent. I needed to hear the story in case I could find a way to fix it all. I didn't want to be mad at Pete. Even though his work issues constantly bombarded my ever-doubting heart, I liked him in my life.

Naturally, I sat down on the sofa. But I moved away from Pete and turned to face him. My knees formed an impenetrable barrier between us, I thought.

"When I saw you that first time. In the cafe." He rubbed the hair at his crown again. "After that, I came home and started writing. I'd been blocked for a while. My editor, John, was jubilant."

I frowned at him. I was listening but not understanding this writing he was talking about. They have editors? Freelancers get writer's block? I assumed they got excited about the next job where they're told what to write.

"Okay. So you hunted me down to keep me around for inspiration. Is that it?"

"Oh, no, no, no. That is not what happened at all. The pet adoption meeting was accidental. I didn't think I'd ever see you again. But I got lucky."

"Lucky. Right. Time to go. See ya, Pete."

I stood and tried to turn away from him, but my shoe stuck weirdly under the coffee table. Turning made me lose my balance. Pete caught my arm. I found myself against his chest, looking up into his eyes. My heart did a flip.

His beautiful eyes. He had tears. Real ones. Not the fake kind Daddy cried. With his thumb, he wiped away the tears on my cheek.

"All of this was much more than luck, Sylvie. I was meant to find you again."

Dipping my head away from his tearful gaze, I broke the spell his magical words were trying to weave.

"Lemme go," I whispered, battling back a wave of nausea.

I don't remember how I got out of his house and into my car. I pulled away from the curb and idled at a stop sign a few blocks down. The dam broke hard. I hadn't realized how much I'd been holding back in his house. All of my muscles sagged. My body prickled everywhere it touched the seat. I couldn't move—afraid of the pain moving would cause.

Eventually, I pulled my forehead off the steering wheel and wiped my hands down my face. That reminded me of Pete wiping my cheek with his thumb. My throat was scorched, and I couldn't bear to feel any more tears burn through my body.

"Woo…" I let out a long breath.

The air shuddered as it passed by my broken heart. It's true. I'd surrendered my heart to that man. Allowed him in my life and let his caring attentiveness cut through my resistance and doubt.

Focus, Sylvie, focus, whispered through my head.

I pounded the steering wheel with my right hand. The vibration skittered up through my shoulder. I closed my eyes to the truth falling in front of me like bricks.

I cannot believe I fell for his crap. He was sneaky like my daddy, but I'd never detected it. The lessons delivered in my childhood home had come to roost.

Unreliable men do unreliable things, and if you let them into your heart, they break you.

Into a million shards of glass.

Chapter 22

Pete

I could kill John. Well, not literally.

And if I'm honest with myself, it's not his fault at all. It's mine. I handled Sylvie all wrong.

Out of potentially a million correct things I could have done, I chose none of those options. They weren't even within my intellectual or emotional grasp. Watching the emotions and doubt play across Sylvie's face broke me. And I didn't know what to do with that empty feeling. But *empty* doesn't come close to expressing the great chasm of loss that stretched across my heart. I thought I'd break in two when she walked out the door.

"Sylvie, don't…" I called after her, but the firm closing of my front door ended my plea. It was Evelyn all over again—another closing door.

What did I have to offer her, anyway? She had her opinions about men, from what I could tell, then lumped me in with some odd group she avoided.

"Stop it, man," I growled at myself. Placing the blame on Sylvie was inexcusable.

Maybe John was at least partly right. I'd hitched my wagon on John's "muse" theory because it served me too well. Oh, the lies we tell ourselves.

Had I kept Sylvie in my life so I could keep on writing? I didn't believe it. My time with Sylvie fed something beyond my writer's spirit. She had turned out to be so much more than a muse. She'd become a special part of this Christmas season. And my life.

I have always loved Christmas. My boyhood excitement had morphed, as I aged, into the sacred. The season always reminds me to slow down a little, think about others more than myself.

It was doubtful Sylvie would ever buy that theory of me. She believed me to be a lying loser who used her for his own gain.

My attraction to her overrode any logical interest in using her for inspiration. That was my story and I was sticking to it. Any reasonable person would believe me, I was certain.

I spotted her at that cafe and my writing took off. Had I not accidentally bumped into her at the dog adoption event, perhaps I'd still have been writing like an inspired genius. Inspired by the beautiful young woman in an ill-fitting red blouse. Surely that was true.

I'd convinced myself, and now I had to persuade Sylvie of this wholesome truth. We could not leave this budding relationship on the rocks. I could not let it go. I wouldn't let her go without a fight.

My text messages went unanswered over the two days leading up to Christmas. I figured she'd fled to Alabama, to be with her family and friends, to tend her wounds.

I called twice and left voicemails both times. I'd have left more, but I've written enough crime stories to know how not to enter stalker territory. My messages were brief but heartfelt.

"Sylvie, you know who this is. The guy you've spent time with these past few weeks is a real guy who cares about you. Please don't end us this way. Merry Christmas."

Us. As if there ever was an us. People in true, healthy relationships are authentic and honest. I never lied to Sylvie, and I revealed true feelings to her. Yet she didn't know who I really was. I had sincerely believed she didn't have to know about my career or my actual house. It would all come out in due time, or we'd no longer be in each other's lives at some future point. That's how I'd handled my conversations with Sylvie.

To be fair, to me, Sylvie didn't ask much about my life, which was strange in itself. Many women I've known were excessively curious about the minutest details of my life. I never wondered about Sylvie's lack of curiosity because I was kinda relieved not to have to explain anything. I figured she was dealing with her broken wrist and the accompanying pain; then add the stress of working solo in a strange city. Besides, her boss seemed like a genuine piece of work, pushing her to keep going after her bone break.

I didn't tell Mom about the fight with Sylvie. We spent Christmas Day together, from breakfast through dinner at her house. Riley and I arrived about ten in the morning.

"I guess Sylvie's in Alabama, huh?"

"I suppose she's having a good time with family, yeah." I avoided Mom's gaze, certain she'd see the pain in my eyes. Nor did I want to encourage her to ask more questions about things I didn't understand myself.

"Did you two exchange gifts before she left? Or is that too soon to happen?"

"Maybe when she comes back. We'll see."

I set down my coffee mug with a clunk on the

kitchen table. Mom had been studying me and discomfort coursed through me. I suppose the dark shadows on my sleep-deprived face were a giveaway to something being wrong. Terribly wrong, indeed.

"Should we open gifts now?"

"Oh, Pete-y, you're like a kid. Sure, let's. These dishes will wait."

I felt like a rotten teen who wanted to avoid helping with cleanup. I had to chuckle.

"Just so you know, I am not trying to avoid helping in the kitchen like when I was fifteen."

After I took Riley out in Mom's back yard, we settled in front of the fire in the den to exchange presents. I'd scrambled for another gift for Mom when it became clear that I couldn't give Riley away. He was my little pal now. If I'd listened to Sylvie from the start, I'd have accepted that reality sooner.

Mom was great with the dog, but she treated him like a grandchild. He had an upset stomach the day after Christmas from all the junk she fed him. I didn't have the heart to stop her.

Watching Mom with Riley made me think about giving her a grandbaby. I was nowhere close to that state of being. Having made a mess of things first with Evelyn and now with Sylvie, I would presumably continue to disappoint my mom in that arena.

Thankfully, Mom asked no more questions about Sylvie. I suspected she was as taken with Sylvie as I was, and her silence on the subject was surprising. Perhaps she had a sense about things. Mom was there for me when Evelyn left, and I shared a lot back then. More than a son probably should have. She was the only person I could share with. Most of my friends were married and settled, unable to console their divorced pal in the ways I needed. If I'd had a female friend or two, I might have received more sympathy.

"Lost" barely describes the person who rambled around my big house then, alone and angry. After a month of maddening silence, Mom barged in. She spent nights, cooked breakfasts, stocked my freezer with meals, and listened to my depressing diatribes about relationships.

This Christmas, I wasn't sure I had much to share about Sylvie. And I wouldn't put a damper on our wonderful day together. Mom didn't need me to spoil one of her favorite days of the year. She always says my birthday is her most favorite one.

Sylvie and I had grown close in some respects, but my sense of our time together was warped. Having Sylvie nearby, yet at arm's length, kept me in an emotional war I'd waged willingly. My attraction to her spirit and her beauty had been in mortal combat with my need to stay detached and uncommitted.

I'd told myself some incredible fiction, that was for darn sure.

No motherly advice was going to fix this thing. It was all on me.

Back at my apartment on Christmas night, sleep again would not come, so I got on the Internet and searched for flights to Birmingham. I'd go find her and grovel if I must. Maybe I'd even do it in front of her entire family. Getting direct flights out of Richmond can be dicey depending on the destination. Weird flight times and long layovers in cities like Chicago sobered my mind. I was being irrational. "Stalker territory," I reminded myself.

Besides, the look on Sylvie's face when she left reminded me that I was ill-equipped to climb over the hill of emotional debris I'd created. Winning her back was a battle I couldn't win overnight. Waiting for something to happen wasn't my strong suit, but patient I had to be.

I just needed to figure out how to get Sylvie talking to me. Texting and calling had failed me. I was thoroughly at a loss.

So I kept writing.

Chapter 23

Sylvie

"I'm ignoring them all."

"Oh, hon," Angie was badgering me once again to reply to Pete. She rallied around Pete's desperate attempts to reach me.

Yes, he was desperate. Or he sounded so. His second voicemail went like this:

"Sylvie, please. Yes, I am actually begging. We need to talk. I'd rather talk in person, look you in the eye and tell you the God's honest truth. But right now, I just want to hear your voice. Um…and know you're okay. I'm not okay, just so you know. I guess you can…"

My voicemail cut him off because he went too long, I guess. At least he didn't call me back to finish his pleading. Hearing his voice hurt like heck. I really wanted to cuss up a storm. I also wanted to talk to him, so I'd quit being confused about his life. Searching for him online hadn't given me anything useful. I think the rental address messed with the search results. It hurt too much to type his name in the search bar, so I gave up.

Angie said my name and brought me back to earth. "Sylvie, honey, I hurt with you."

I sniffled and rubbed my forearm across my nose. I looked at my green sweater sleeve. No harm done. I didn't care what I looked like for work today.

"Thanks, Angie, for listening to my wailing. I feel

so sick. Lunch on Christmas Day was my only meal in two days."

"Wish I hadn't eaten in two days. My mama has been baking up a storm. And I stop in the kitchen every time I pass through. But it's not the same thing. You really shouldn't be starvin' yourself."

"It's okay. Maybe I'll get my thigh gap back." I checked my legs in the mirror.

"That's my girl. Making jokes, now that's healthy."

I pulled back a heavy brocade curtain and looked out the hotel room window. The sky hung low with flat, gray clouds. I shivered. Flat and gray matched my mood. I couldn't get warm, even snuggled under the hotel covers.

"How was it being in Nashville for Christmas Day?" Angie kept the conversation going at her end to keep me from descending into more sadness.

"It was fine. A little lonely. The hotel had a delicious buffet for the guests. The change of scenery is what I desperately need, though. I chatted with my parents and sister. It's all good. I'll have a pile of gifts waiting for me whenever I get back home, so there's that."

"I shoulda called you yesterday. I'm sorry."

"Hey, no biggie. It was Sunday. You had family stuff all day. However, I'd have loved to be home to see you and your crazy gang. I missed you all the most, I think."

Storm clouds gathered in my head, and my eyes threatened to rain. I took a deep breath.

"I miss you too, my dear Sylvie. You're the bestest friend."

"I dunno about that. It's been all 'me, me, me' lately. What's been going on with Flirtable and that last fellow you mentioned?"

"Eh. I dunno. I had to put him off till after Christmas. The shop nearly ran me ragged. Scratch that—the shop DID run me into the ground! I'm exhausted. But no rest, cuz now it's almost inventory time."

Angie sighed so loudly I could almost envision her shoulders slumping.

"Well, at least you have two fellows dangling out there."

"True enough. More than I've had for a while."

"Need to get to work, my friend. Both of us do. Patrick wanted me in the office by nine today. That's not gonna happen if I don't get a move on."

Patrick infuriated me when he informed me a week before Christmas that I needed to be at corporate offices on December 27. What a Grinch, I'd thought. And a jerk. His request would cut short my trip home, a hoped-for surprise for my family. I'd planned to head there soon after I left Pete's place four days ago. The worst part was my plan had also included traveling with a cheerful heart after helping Pete decorate the tree and maybe other rooms in his apartment.

As I dragged my sorrowful self into my apartment, I got a call from Victoria, who was checking on me before the holiday. The season decimated her volunteer ranks, yet she took time to check on how I was healing. So sweet of her.

I wasn't very chatty, and she picked up on that. I couldn't explain the hurt I was feeling right after leaving Pete's. So I only told her that Pete and I had a falling out. She sounded disappointed when she said, "I'm so sorry, Sylvie." She had the wisdom not to take sides or convince me to rethink my reaction, like Angie would have done. Victoria and I were in a different friendship spot, and I enjoyed that lack of probing when I was raw with heartbreak.

After talking to Victoria, I called the airline and changed my ticket so I could fly to Nashville the next day, on Christmas Eve.

I cried myself to sleep that night. Ignoring all of Pete's texts.

Lying in bed, I replayed all the moments we had shared in just a few short weeks. His face crinkled with laughter, the warmth of his voice—and those silly flannel shirts swam before my eyes. The memories made me smile, but then I'd start sniffling again. My nose was stopped up, but I cradled a box of tissues anyway. My eyes burned from hours of crying, and I hoped that I'd run out of the salty tears before I left town.

I chose to go to Nashville instead of Birmingham because I could not show up at my parents' in such a dreadful state. I know myself and Momma. We'd never make it twenty-four hours before I fell into an emotional heap on the kitchen floor. The kitchen is Momma's home during the holidays. I don't think she gets but a few hours of sleep a night between Thanksgiving and Christmas. I refused to become a shredded rug under her feet.

Being on my own for a few days had made avoiding thoughts of Pete beyond hard. I went to church yesterday to help fill my third day alone. They still included Christmas songs in the service and that made me miss Pete more. I'd been carrying around a mental broom to sweep away every errant thought that tried to creep into my brain, like when I remembered his dark eyes on me. All the while I believed he had feelings for me, he'd been watching me for writing inspiration.

Angie had looked up *muse* and told me all about the history and how the whole thing was supposed to work. She'd teased me about being a goddess. Huh! I shook my head for the umpteenth time.

I stood in front of the bathroom mirror and put on my makeup. Dark shadows defied all my attempts to brighten my eyes, so a haunted look remained. Thank goodness the pink puffiness was gone. Nothing I did with my makeup brush tamed the sadness that tarnished my features.

I hoped to find Patrick in his usual distracted, self-involved mode—not something I wished for often. He could be hard to follow on a good day, bouncing around ideas. Being in meetings with Patrick often felt like we stood on opposing sides of a ping-pong table. Kept me on my toes. I'll say that about his management style.

I wouldn't be setting up a new location for the company if I hadn't kept up with him in his rapid-fire staff meetings. But he had me wondering about the urgency of this command appearance in Nashville. He'd been rather vague about the purpose of the coming days' meetings with clients. These weren't my clients, who were hundreds of miles away, so why was I asked to be here? Not *asked*, but *told* to be in Nashville. Two days after Christmas. Most people would wait until the new year, wouldn't they?

I growled at my reflection in the mirror, seeing Patrick's face instead.

****

By lunchtime, I still didn't know why I was there. Patrick had started the day with a two-hour discussion—he called it a "deep dive." His love for the business jargon that I'd heard mocked during my MBA studies was a little irritating. One might think I didn't like my boss, but I do. He's just got a few quirks, I guess you'd call them. He's demanding and has a low regard for other people's lives and the impact that real life has on workflow and all.

Still, he hadn't asked why I looked like I'd been run over by a truck, so his low score on the caring-for-others scale served me well. Patrick was a study in contrasts. Even though he came across as somewhat uncaring in the day-to-day stuff, he was quite the charmer. How does one rise to the top of a consulting business without a whole lotta charm to win over new clients? One does not, so let's just say Patrick could charm the coat off a freezing man. He's that good.

He's also quite good-looking. Not as hot as Pete, but... There I went, thinking about Pete again. Would I ever rid my heart of his memory? It sure didn't feel like I could file him away; not for now, at least.

Anyway, Patrick has a thin face made up of all kinds of interesting angles, and his blond hair, well... It's so blond, it's like his mother poured heavy cream on his head. He stands out wherever he goes. Patrick looks good for a guy nearing fifty, that's all I can say. And he's a nice dresser, which he can afford. He's been managing this business for at least two decades, I think.

The morning involved just the two of us, with me briefing on all my client work from the past six months. I did the "deep dive" while Patrick nodded and steepled his fingers together. I'd finally made a strong showing in Richmond, so I had a chance to shine. Patrick was complimentary, to my relief. I needed a bright spot.

More staff filtered in for a larger meeting which met over lunch. Sandwiches, snacks, and drinks covered a pale wooden credenza that looked Scandinavian. I found the furnishings style in this office a little odd for Nashville, but that's Patrick for you. A little off-kilter and mismatched with the world around him! Haha, I'm so funny.

After that meeting, I got caught up with some of the staff I'd worked with when I lived in Nashville. The IT guy had to walk me through a new system the company was launching. They put me in a huge corner office where I could make calls to a couple of my Richmond clients. I didn't know who the office belonged to, but it may have been unclaimed. The company's business suite had grown, taking over the rest of the space on the tenth floor of the building when another tenant moved out. The views of the city were gorgeous and distracting, and I could get used to working there.

Patrick called me into his office for a private meeting late in the afternoon. I wondered what we would discuss, given we'd spent hours together that morning. Whatever, I thought. No telling what he had up his sleeve.

However, nothing had prepared me for what he had to say. He started talking about confusing things from way out in left field. That was my feeling. It was all so unexpected and farfetched. Even for Patrick.

Chapter 24

Pete

My phone rang, and I answered the unknown number. Unusual for me and most everyone on the planet, I'm sure. But it was an Alabama number, so I had to answer it. I hadn't heard from Sylvie since she left my place five days ago.

All my calls went to voicemail. I knew she'd never let me in, so I didn't even try to go by her place. I owed her an over-the-top gesture, but the holidays had stymied me. Plus, I'd finished my novel's first draft. Yep, I did it without Sylvie around to inspire me.

Christmas had come and gone. I guessed she was working in Nashville.

"Pete?" A woman's voice with an accent stronger than Sylvie's chirped over the airwaves.

"Yes?"

"Hi Pete, you don't know me, but I suppose Sylvie told you about her best friend, Angie. That's me. She gave me your number back when she hurt her arm."

"Yeah, she told me about you, Angie. Um, I haven't spoken to her in a few days. Have you?"

"Well…she's in Nashville."

"Right. How is she? We haven't—"

"I heard. I'm brokenhearted myself, cuz ya'll sounded like the perfect match. Sylvie may have been a cheerleader when we were kids, but I was your

177

cheerleader these past weeks." Angie sighed.

"I appreciate that. How is she doing? What can you tell me?" I looked across the living room. The tree Sylvie had left behind stood naked on the speaker in the corner. I had kept it watered, at least. But it made me feel like such a jerk. Had I blown it for good? I was desperate for any chance to make things right with Sylvie.

"Her boss has kept her real busy, you know. Work all day, dinner out every night. It's been a whirlwind. He's trying to woo her."

What? I drove a hand through my hair. This could not be happening.

"Woo her?" My voice squeaked at the end. I shook out my free arm and rolled my shoulders to release the tension.

"Yeah, back to Nashville at the home office. Offering her this amazing corner office and she'll get to hire her own assistant. Who wouldn't be interested in that?"

"I see. And she's entertaining this…idea?" I wanted to say *stupid idea* but bit my tongue.

"Maybe a little. She has more ties there than in Richmond. She left a boyfriend—that was Andrew—behind when she moved. Well, they weren't together when she left, but he's still there. Plus, all the people at Montross who she was close to."

"Hmm. Can I ask why you've called to share all this?"

"Light a fire under you! That's why!"

"Sylvie doesn't know you're calling me, I take it." I walked to my bedroom and started throwing clothes onto the bed.

"Good Lord, no. She'd kill me. But death would be

worth it if y'all got back together."

Together. Had we actually been together? I wanted to believe we had been headed in the same direction. We'd spent most of our energy holding back. What Sylvie's reasoning was, I could only guess.

Me? I was just plain afraid. I didn't want to nurse a broken heart ever again, but here I was tending to one anyway.

"Thank you, thank you, Angie. You're a peach. A perfect Georgia peach."

"Aww, yer welcome. So…did it work? Is the fire lit?"

I laughed.

"Fire started. I've got some stuff to do. Hopefully, you'll find out about it soon."

"Yes!"

"I gotta run, Angie. But thank you so much. I hope I get to meet you in person one day."

"Me too! Bye!"

I tossed my phone onto the dresser. I rubbed a hand down my face and noticed I needed to shave. I had too much to do and no time.

I started with the airlines. I booked a one-way ticket to Nashville. Called a car service, so I didn't have to park and wait on a shuttle up to the gate. Hopped in the shower, shaved, dressed.

I packed all the clean clothes I had. Most of my clothes remained at my house, as I'd yet to go get some warmer things. My contractor had given me a Christmas present, though, promising me I could move back after the first week of January. Ten more days.

I had fewer days to get Sylvie back to my city. Spending New Year's Eve with her was my goal.

Riley wandered in to see what all the commotion was about, I suppose.

"Riley, boy. Geez Louise!"

What was I going to do with my little friend? I looked at my watch and made a call.

****

I'd texted Angie for Sylvie's hotel. Her response had been a row of happy face emoji's and then the hotel name. I'm sure I looked ridiculous grinning at my phone, waiting to board at the Richmond airport gate.

Outside the airport in Nashville, I flagged a cab at the curb. "Midtown Hotel, please."

I was headed toward the woman I wanted to learn everything about. Too much about her remained a mystery, and we'd danced around important questions we were too afraid to give voice to.

The past few days had been awash with feelings of loss like I couldn't recall ever experiencing before. Not even at the end of my marriage to Evelyn. But I'd finished my draft, even without my muse nearby. It was done. For now, anyway. I'd look at it again in the new year.

But first things first. Sylvie.

I walked into the cherry wood warmth of the hotel. Without a plan. Do I sit in the lobby and wait for her to appear? Call her room? Or maybe call or text her cell and say, "Surprise, I'm here!"

The lobby welcomed guests with rich wood and marble columns. Honey gold streaked across white marble on the floors. A man's voice sang about a beach while I checked in at reception. I supposed the Christmas music had been removed from the rotation already. Pity.

I got my keycard and headed for the bank of

180

elevators. As I passed the pub-style restaurant off the lobby, I slowed down when I saw Sylvie's dark blonde hair swishing across female shoulders. The woman tossed her head back in raucous laughter. Not the woman I couldn't wait to see.

What I would do when I had her attention, I wasn't sure. Maybe it would come to me the minute I saw her. I could write similar scenes in my books, but I couldn't write my own.

I found my room on the seventh floor, close to the elevators. I sat on the bed and took a deep breath.

My phone was in my hand, so I pulled her info up. Then I just stared at it.

"C'mon, Pete. Get a grip."

It was six in the evening on a Wednesday. She was probably at dinner. With her boss. Or that Andrew guy?

I scowled at my reflection in the mirror. I had no one to blame for this disaster but myself. She got away because I was a coward. Too stupid and scared to be honest about my feelings when it counted.

Sure, I tried the other night. It was too little, too late. I stumbled all over, trying to fix the muse story while walking the yellow line of caution around my true feelings. When all was said and done, Sylvie got hurt and it was my fault.

Was I going to keep beating myself up over my stubbornness, or do something about her? I was here, wasn't I? I had that going for me, but I had to figure out how to leverage this trip into a permanent result.

Permanent? Was I honestly ready for commitment to Sylvie? Gosh, that woman had messed with my entire life. I ran my hand across my head and gazed around the room. My eyes landed on the black faux-leather portfolio on the desk. Room service menu inside?

I was a little hungry but didn't feel like leaving the room. Did I fear running into Sylvie without a warning? What if she was with someone? What a fool I was.

Chastised, I still didn't leave the room. I called room service, splashed my face with cold water, and leaned back against the pillows till my dinner arrived.

A knock jarred me out of my sleep. I rubbed my eyes, slowly realizing where I was. Nashville. I shouldn't be surprised I took a nap, given I'd slept poorly since Sylvie walked out. Was that five nights ago?

I groaned as I swung my sleep-laden legs to a standing position.

"Coming," I spoke to the person on the other side of the golden oak door.

I gave the hotel server a big smile as he entered and rolled the cart beside a small table near the window. I saw only our images in the glass—darkness and city lights on the other side. Handing him a cash tip, I nodded and closed the door on the quiet hallway.

The scents coming from the corner lured me over. The burger glistened under the light. I snagged a fat fry and folded it into my salivating mouth. After spreading a white linen napkin over my jeans, I tucked into my dinner with a vengeance.

I pushed every thought of Sylvie out of my head and focused on my meal. The silence filled the gaping spaces around me and my hurting heart, and I found a peace I hadn't had for a while.

I pulled the curtains shut against flashing red neon announcing honky-tonk music and beer. It was time for me to figure out how to salvage this apparently misbegotten trip. Taking a plane to a city I'd never visited was out of my comfort zone, unless I was traveling for a book-signing. During those, I'm rarely in charge and just go with the flow.

Sylvie was my comfort zone; I'd learned that. A woman may not like to hear she's comfortable, but in Sylvie I found a place of contentment. She'd become home to me, a resting place where I could just be.

I was adrift and lost at sea. How could I find her and get us on the same page? How persuadable would she be? Had time away given her a new perspective, one that would be open to starting over again with a stupid, scared man? Or was she done with me?

Too many questions, no answers.

As I was placing my dinner cart outside my door, my phone buzzed. I couldn't believe the screen when I slid the vibrating phone out of my pocket.

Chapter 25

Sylvie

Patrick, my boss, kept me busy with new staff and in meetings every minute. At night, he wined and dined me along with some of his newest clients. How he'd pulled them away from home over this holiday week, I couldn't imagine. The bar bills alone were huge, so that could've been part of the allure.

By the third day at work, I couldn't stop yawning. I needed to return to Richmond. Not that I have much there, based on Patrick's final summation of my office. He didn't insult me exactly. No, he had nothing but good things to say about the Richmond effort, and my success had given him a gleam in his eye. A lot of mixed messages, to say the least.

He had brought me back to the main office to promote me and install me in the Nashville office. The title and pay raise he offered filled my head with a few grand dreams. He had a couple of new hires he planned to send to Richmond in my place.

I found it tempting. But I was also possessive of my clients and the work I'd done in Richmond.

Besides, my favorite time of year had been ruined by the disappointment delivered by Pete. Maybe I overreacted and I should have heard him out.

Maybe, maybe. That's all I got for Christmas this year—a not-so-shiny box of self-doubt.

I scrolled through my photo files for a picture of little Riley. I'd made the little fella my phone's lock screen picture, too. That dog had grabbed my heart in his paws. His brown eyes stared out at me. Behind him, I noticed Pete's hand. Unable to help myself, I scrolled through my photos and found one of Pete hanging an ornament on my tree.

I found another photo, a selfie I took of us in front of that fabulous Christmas tree at that beautiful hotel. I was looking directly at the camera, but Pete's gaze was on me. He'd been laughing and saying something about selfies.

My nose burned as tears formed. I decided to text him and ask about Riley. I had no good reason to do it. I remained miffed about the whole writing muse thing. Felt a little used. But a part of me recognized—with some certainty—Pete actually cared about me. That photo told a story I could not unread.

I found Pete's contact and accidentally hit the call button. Before I made the conscious decision to hang up, I heard Pete's, "Hello?"

"Hi. Pete. Um. Sorry to just call out of the blue. I meant to—"

"No, I'm glad you called…how are you?"

I grimaced at the phone. What the heck was I doing? The sound of his voice caused my heart to race.

"Well, I really meant to text you and ask about Riley. How's the little fella doing?"

"Good. He had a good Christmas…for a dog."

I pictured Pete running a hand across the top of his head. I had bought a gift for Riley before—

"I'm sorry to bother you. Um, I'm still in Nashville."

"No bother. You've never bothered me, Sylvie."

I heard an apology, or sadness, in his voice. My heart lurched across the phone line. I wanted to be in Richmond right now.

I laughed nervously.

"Can I see you?"

Pete's voice whispered into my ear. I wanted to scream "yes," but I wasn't sure I'd feel the same way when I got back in a couple of days. A weariness brought on by massive over-stimulation from Patrick's meetings and schemes infused every cell of my body. To call the week a whirlwind would be a vast understatement.

"Um, well, Pete. I won't be back till late on New Year's Eve."

"What if I were in Nashville?"

"You'd come to Nashville? But I'm leaving soon!"

"Sylvie…" He paused, and I braced myself to hear an apology or something awful, like an excuse. "I'm here. In Nashville. I hoped to find you."

I held my palm flat against my forehead. My eyes twitched and lightheadedness swam over me.

"You did? Wow! Um, I don't know what to say, but…" That was the truth. I had no response to hearing he'd come here to find me. I mean, who does that?

People in love? Possibly. I hated the uncertainty that had clouded everything since I met Pete. Yes, I had wanted something with him, and while it had taken me time to stop denying my feelings, I was startled that I might let him waltz right back in. Back into my heart—my aching, broken heart.

I wasn't honest with Angie about why I hadn't eaten much in two days. The minute I checked into this hotel room, I put on my pajamas and crawled into bed. My eyes had been hot with tears and grief, yet I'd shivered under the covers.

Living in Alabama, I'd seen the devastation of a hurricane. Pictures flooded the television news the two times our coast got hit in my short lifetime. Trees stripped bare, their branches gnarled by the sheer force of wind and water. On a trip to the beach a couple of years ago, I saw the damage to an oak—the mightiest of trees—up close. Sections of its trunk were bare, and the exposed wood was slick and scarred—kinda like my heart.

I'd allowed my heart to be hammered by Hurricane Love, which probably isn't a fair metaphor for a broken heart. Or maybe it is? Hurricanes are usually expected, but every locality has at least one stalwart citizen who refuses to budge. They plan to hunker down and sit it out, or whatever they tell the local police. They'll be fine, they're certain. No urgent warnings convince them to pack up and get the heck out of Dodge.

I had done the same with Pete. I let him into my life and wandered along the path of the storm. Alarm bells rang and my checklist shook itself in front of my face, and I ended up drowning beneath a tsunami of tears and regret.

Betrayal is a gruesome thing. Pete had betrayed my trust. But I had also betrayed myself and my list—my stupid checklist. Who had betrayed my heart the most— Pete or me? All these questions sent me into hours of tears and thrashing in the hotel bed. I'd eventually run out of sadness, though the only thing that filled the empty space was loneliness.

"Say you'll meet for a drink. I know it's late. I'm at the Midtown Hotel, downtown."

"Me too! That's super weird. The pub at nine?"

"I'll be there."

"Wait. Pete?"

"Yeah?"

"What did you do with Riley?"

He chuckled, of course. Gosh, I'd missed that sound.

"Fair question. Your friend Victoria did me a favor. She's keeping him."

"Well, aren't you a charmer." I smirked.

"She likes you…and me too, I guess."

"I guess she does."

"See you in a few, then?" Pete asked.

"Yes, see you in a few."

He hung up.

I sat on the edge of my bed, fingers curled tightly around my phone. Everything fluttered. My heart bounced in my chest. I rejected the automatic impulse to call Angie. I had to write this scene on my own, with only my words, and Pete's, on the page.

What am I doing? I asked myself for the hundredth time since meeting this handsome, caring man.

Pete and I had tiptoed around each other. Why he was afraid of me, I didn't know. I only knew he held back most of the time, which belied the interested looks I caught him sending my way. We were both guilty. Of being stupid, scared, and sad.

Yes, sad. I had been miserable since the day I left Pete's place, experiencing days and days of misery. Nothing stopped the thoughts crowding my brain— remembering how protected he made me feel. His nurturing nature had blurred my vision of the checklist, and I didn't know how to categorize him anymore.

Pete sounded unhappy, too. He said he'd "hoped" to

find me. He came to Nashville for…me? And ended up in the same hotel.

I checked the time on my phone. Twenty minutes until truth time. What was the truth, anyway? What did I want? Did Pete want the same things as me? Assuming I knew anything about those kinds of wants. I sighed as I dusted loose powder over my face.

Earlier in the evening, Patrick had chosen a restaurant within walking distance of my hotel, but I'd begged off as soon as I politely could. Weary and relieved that I didn't have to listen to Patrick drone on for the fourth night in a row, I'd strolled back to my room. But on the way in, I'd dropped into a cushy club chair and listened to the lobby pianist play some old tunes for a group of older women. They were cute and made me miss my Momma.

Even so, I was back in my room early. A tiny reason to celebrate, but instead I became morose about how things went down in Richmond. I missed little Riley and hit the wrong button on the phone. And then I made a drink date. I groaned over my foolish memories. My thumb hovered over my phone, the idea of canceling heavy on my heart. I looked at the photo of Pete and me again, examining it for a hint of anything but affection on Pete's face. Regrets would abound if I didn't keep this date, of that I was certain.

Suddenly, I was certain of something, until I had to head downstairs.

I debated arriving early and establishing myself at a table with a drink I'd paid for. Or maybe I should make an entrance. My resolve floundered. I buried my head in my hands and breathed deeply.

I nixed the entrance idea. Definitely not my style.

I punched the elevator button and stood stiffly, waiting for the ubiquitous "ding" of the elevator, stopping on my floor. My reflection in the steel doors didn't reassure me—pale, tired. I was the same inside and out. The elevator doors opened, and I stepped into the empty box.

I'd taken only two deep stress-filled breaths when the elevator opened again into the noisy lobby. I could do this. I was about to see Pete after six days.

The hum of disjointed voices in the bar reached the elevator doors. Clinking glasses and laughter filtered out into the lobby as I approached the pub. I scanned the tables I could see—no Pete.

A smiling hostess in a strapless black dress that ended above her knees greeted me. I held up two fingers, and she picked up two menus, gesturing that I follow.

"Is this okay?" She nodded at a high-top table in a corner.

"Perfect. Thanks. I'm meeting a man. Tall, dark hair."

I couldn't see the entrance, so I spent the next few minutes scanning the crowded restaurant for Pete. I ordered a drink and waited. Why was he really in Nashville?

Half of me was excited to see him, the other half still angry. Not angry, I suppose, but a bit haunted. The sound of that man's voice on Pete's phone replayed in my head whenever I beckoned it. He "kept me around" so he could write. Writing what I'd never tried to figure out.

I'd done some important writing when I wrote him off. The plane lifted off from Richmond and my heart said farewell.

Yet there I sat, waiting to get a glimpse of the man

who broke my heart.

Pete materialized between two tables, smiling at people as he ducked around them. His smile faltered when he locked his eyes on mine. I stayed still as a statue.

"Sylvie." Pete stopped behind the leather stool across from me.

"Hi." My mouth was so dry, I took a quick sip of my wine. Perhaps he'd buy into the nonchalant air I was going for.

Raucous laughter roared behind me, and I jumped.

"We can go somewhere else." Pete sat and leaned both forearms on the table, cool as a cucumber.

"This is fine." I smiled tentatively, unsure of myself. Unsure of Pete and why we were there. The workday and this mystery had tired me out. I folded my hands together and looked him straight in the eye.

"Why are you in Nashville?"

And, of course, he ran his hand across the top of his dark hair and scratched his crown. I sat still and waited. My insides turned to jelly. He looked too good. But his eyes betrayed the wariness I wanted him to experience. The mean part of me thought I deserved a wary Pete who was unsure of me.

"You."

"Came a long way to not say much."

Pete snorted, which he often did at my pithy humor.

"Angie called me, to be honest."

I said nothing, surprised by my friend's assertiveness. But should I have been?

"Okay. I know you think I wasn't honest with you, but…" He ran a hand over his jaw and shook his head when I frowned.

"Guess I should've written this down."

"In my college composition class, my professor advised starting with what you really want to say."

"Look, Sylvie…" Pete took a deep breath. "I fell for you. Hard. Being around you, watching you with Riley, the past month has been the best time I've had in years. But I let my fear keep me in denial. That's what I needed to say. In person."

"You have this wall around you. I didn't think I was allowed in. To be honest, I wasn't sure if I wanted us to be closer."

"Okay, some more honesty. My divorce, it…" He shook his head. "I've been a wounded soldier limping around for the last five years. You were like a Red Cross nurse tending to me, only you didn't have any idea of the pleasure…what pure pleasure it's been to meet you. To be with you."

Surprising myself, I reached across the table and touched his hand. He twined his fingers with mine. I hoped my eyes beamed some empathy his way. I loved the warmth of his hand in mine but still wasn't sure this was right. Yet being there felt so perfect. Did I mention my head was in a jumble?

"I left you a couple of voicemails."

"And a massive number of texts."

"Were you going to let all this—us—go?"

"I—I've been terribly confused. About what I want from a relationship. I've been working off a checklist since college, trying to find the perfect man, I suppose."

"Keeps you focused. I get it."

"I also didn't tell you a lot about me. We've both made some mistakes. My dad's so unreliable. Life at home was not always financially stable. I mean, for a relationship to work, to have a life together, people have to have steady jobs, and…" I could never tell him I wished he had a better job. His life looked perfect in a slightly warped way.

"So you're saying I need a steady job? Okay." Pete chuckled.

"No, no. You made me realize that my stupid checklist is wrong. It's ridiculous and unfair. You're clearly devoted to your writing, and I should learn more about it. And about you. You have…I don't know…upended my world?"

He rubbed a thumb over my palm, and a smile teased the corners of his mouth. He had something to say, but he clamped his lips together instead.

I asked him about his mom and their Christmas. I told him about my work in Nashville and my plans for returning to Richmond. He held my hand the entire time, and I couldn't stop smiling at him.

And then I yawned.

"Whoa. I'm boring you."

"Sorry. I've just had a brutal day. Three of them, to be exact." I stifled another yawn. "And this has been an emotional night. Seeing you."

"Thank you for saying 'yes.'"

"Thank you for finding me, and you came all this way. I'm truly overwhelmed." I teared up, and I wiped one away. My heartbeat whooshed inside my ears.

"Let's go."

We stopped in the lobby, and I wondered stupidly what floor he was on and how we'd navigate the getting-off-on-our-floor dance.

"Hey." Pete ducked his head to look into my eyes, which were focused on the markings on the marble floor. "Sylvie, two people who love you, Angie and Victoria, are in our corner. They think we have something here. Sleep on that tonight. Please. We *are* great together. I hope you see it too."

I smiled weakly. I could feel the energy leaving me, puddling on the marble floor. With the idea of an "us" with Pete simmering in my gut, I wanted him to kiss me goodnight.

Pete left me there in front of the elevators in the lobby, promising that he'd see me in the morning. I wondered if he really was staying in my hotel, since he didn't get on the elevator with me. I still had trust issues, it seemed.

Snuggled under the covers, I replayed the pub conversation until the early hours. I wished again that Pete had kissed me goodnight in front of the elevators. Finally, I fell asleep.

Chapter 26

Pete

I left Sylvie at the bank of elevators, cut across the marble floors, and out the revolving glass door. Frigid air bit my cheeks and made my eyes water. Well, even the south doesn't escape winter's frosty nip. I popped up the collar of my nearly useless fleece and turned right.

There was a jewelry store nearby, but of course it had closed at nine. Instead, I window shopped, finding something I hoped Sylvie would love. I'd get it in the morning.

If I hadn't been so deep into my book drafting, I might have already bought a gift for Sylvie. But when she bolted before Christmas, finding her a gift fell off my to-do list. I hadn't been very hopeful, to be honest. I couldn't wrap my head or my heart around winning her back.

Call me the prince of lost causes. I give up way too easily when it comes to romance. It was a wonder I married Evelyn. She charged up into my world when I signed with my first publisher. She dragged me into a new life and then marriage. I didn't know what hit me.

And as failure dashed through our union with a one-two punch, I stood stunned against a wall, afraid to move. Been standing there since, watching women walk by, squeezing my eyes shut to opportunity.

When Sylvie sat nearby at my favorite cafe, I

wanted to stop holding up that stupid wall. Why did I fight the falling? The vertigo in my heart was real, and I didn't know how to suppress it.

Was that the truth Sylvie still needed to hear? She seemed open, softened to my presence. Not the distraught woman who fled my house and the city a week ago. I hoped she wasn't playing with me to get another last laugh. Obviously, I still had trust issues.

Early the next morning, I texted Sylvie.

"You up?"

"Of course! Gotta be @ work by 9." She included a tongue-out emoji. I had to laugh. I use that one myself sometimes—mostly about work, too.

"Coffee downstairs in 15?" I crossed my fingers on both hands and stared at the three dots wiggling on the screen.

"Sure."

"By the piano in 15. See ya." Avoid misunderstandings—my new plan.

She didn't text back. I rubbed my head, searching for meaning to the silence. I left my room so I could pace the lobby for fifteen minutes. What a strategy. Granted, I had no strategy. In the wee hours, I'd plotted ideas, then scratched them off the list for a couple of hours till sleep mercifully came.

While sitting on the piano bench, elbows on knees, my eyes carved up the marble floor. Nothing brilliant had emerged from my sleep-deprived brain. I wondered if Sylvie would have similar dark circles under her eyes.

She did not. She stopped in front of my pensive pose, a glimpse of black boots in my line of sight.

"Hey," she said as I lifted my head and smiled up at her.

"Good morning."

I stood and gestured toward the hotel's cafe. Following her, my heart tumbled around my chest.

"Did you sleep well?" I asked as she sat in the black metal chair I held the back of. My mom did try hard to raise a gentleman, though I've failed more times than I care to count.

"Mmm-hmm," she nodded as she picked up a menu. "I'm starved."

"Coffee, to start," I said to the server, who turned to leave.

"I think I'll just have toast."

"I thought you…" I stopped myself from questioning what she'd said before. Not the way to begin this restart. Go with it, Pete, I reminded myself. I put the menu down when the server returned with the coffee, and I ordered our breakfast.

The dark, earthy coffee aroma drifted upward, and I felt revived before the first sip hit my lips. I love most hotel coffee. They typically invest in the best beans. This one didn't disappoint.

"I've been thinking."

"Do tell."

"Well, considering you came all this way to see me, I reckon I should be available. You're here, so…"

Not a rousing endorsement of spending time with me, but I had to take my lumps.

"Ohhh-kay. That would be nice. You being available, I mean. But—"

Sylvie held up her hand.

"I've worked twelve-plus hour days. I should be able to make Patrick see the light. Just give me the morning at the office and I'll text you."

I dabbed a cloth napkin on my mouth and nodded.

"I like the way you think." I held her gaze. "I always have…um, liked the way you think."

I was staring at a paradox. The woman could make me stumble for words when they were about me or her. On the other hand, she had helped release a career-changing word flow from me I hadn't experienced since before Evelyn left me.

"Gotta run." Her hand lingered on my shoulder, and then she walked off. I watched her leave, her gray wool coat flapping with the sway of her hips. She was something else. The warm weight of her handprint remained on my shoulder long after she disappeared.

I played with my eggs and requested more coffee. Twice. I waited for the jewelry store to open and left the hotel.

They didn't have Christmas paper, but the gold paper and ribbon were perfect for this gift. With time to kill, I wandered Nashville's "Broadway" where the twang of music filtered out to the street every time a door opened. My breath was visible, but I was thankful for the subtle warmth of the white sunshine filtering through December clouds.

I maneuvered around the slow walkers on the sidewalk. A woman in white leather head to toe yelled, "Hey, are you PJ Monroe?"

I turned and smiled, still moving and walking backward.

"Yes, ma'am."

She squealed and rushed at me. I laughed out loud, and so did she.

"I appreciate the recognition," I said to her.

"I've read all your books! When's the next one

coming out? Do you live here? Can I—"

I held up a hand to forestall the interrogation.

"Next summer. And I don't live in Nashville." I took her hand in both of mine and thanked her again. And got away. Such is the world of real-life fans who recognize your face. Oh, to be invisible. But then no one would know me and my work. I can't have anonymity and fame at the same time.

With fame comes money. And Sylvie knew nothing about any of that as it relates to me, to my chagrin. In all fairness, it had never popped up in a conversation. But I needed to come clean. I worried how she'd react to another perceived deception.

I ducked into a store and began to plan for the afternoon.

And I didn't see Sylvie until the evening after all. She managed a two-hour early getaway from Patrick, so we'd get to meet earlier for dinner. I'd take that small gift of time. Echoes of Evelyn and one of the main reasons our marriage collapsed.

There's no enjoyment in comparing Sylvie with my ex. I needed to stop and air out my brain. My life's filled with words—what I say, what I write. Not all of it is printable.

"Pete?" A voice from my past wove through the garbled yarns that were my miserable thoughts. My first agent, Kevin Smith, stood in front of me. We'd parted ways when I switched firms early in my career.

"Hey, man!" I stuck out my hand. He pulled me into a bear hug.

"I literally was just thinking about you."

"I hate to ask why." I chuckled. I ducked under an awning to get the sun out of my eyes. How are weak white winter rays so blinding?

"I left Teresa and the kids back at the hotel. Wanna grab a bite?"

I checked my phone to see a sad face emoji from Sylvie. I was on my own for a while longer.

"Sure, sure."

It became clear that my buddy Kevin was avoiding his familial responsibilities. He had three beers to my one. I needed to maintain my senses if I was going to woo Sylvie out of Patrick's grip and back to Richmond.

Forget the muse, I wanted the woman.

A ding on my phone at three in the afternoon provided the escape hatch I needed to end Kevin's long lunch of irresponsibility. After making vague promises to keep in touch, I headed back to the hotel still bearing the jeweler's beautiful gold gift bag and the rest of my shopping.

Chapter 27

Sylvie

I texted Angie during a break from Patrick's endless meetings. She sent me a ridiculous number of happy face and heart emojis when I told her I had seen Pete. My dating life made her act like a seventh grader.

Pete wanted to meet in the pub for a drink so we could decide on dinner together. We'd only eaten out a couple of times—that first Chinese dinner and the place I got pancakes. Plus, the takeout he'd brought over a couple of times. So, I guess you could call it our first date.

Wait a minute. Was it a date? It felt like it. I looked down at my green velvet dress, thankful I had over-packed. Plus, I'd gotten out of work at three so I could rest a little before making myself as beautiful as possible. I wanted to look perfect for him. This was a date, but I had to be sure.

I approached the table where Pete sat reading, and I asked him, "Is this a date?"

His head popped up from the book in his hands. Reading glasses perched on his nose gave him a professorial air. I wished I'd had a professor who looked like him. I'd have been an A student in that course!

"Do you want it to be?" he asked as he removed the glasses and pocketed them.

He wore a blazer. If only it were tweed, I mused. I

pointed a finger at him and drew a circle in the air. "No fair answering a question with a question, Professor!"

"I want it to be a date if that's all right with you. It's kind of our first one, right?"

"Yeah. This is officially our first date."

"I don't know the latest rules, so I have to trust you on the definition of a date."

"Outta practice, huh?"

"Significantly."

"Until I did the online dating thing, I hadn't had a date in well over a year. A professor at the university asked me out after a meeting about interns—that was a one-hit wonder. It's the blind leading the blind, I'm afraid."

"I'm just relieved you're sitting in front of me. And you are beautiful, as always."

His intense gaze held mine. Warmth spread up my neck and face so hot I didn't want to look in any mirror. Just in time, a server appeared with glasses of beer and red wine.

"I took the liberty," Pete said. "Hope you don't mind. Cabernet, right?"

"Thank you," I said as I took a big sip. My nerves had been jangling since last night.

"You're not wearing your brace."

"It's not supposed to be removed till New Year's Day, according to my doctor, but it's been feeling better for a few days. Tonight's my first unbandaged night. Hope I don't regret it. What're you reading?" I leaned over as he flattened a tanned hand across the cover.

"You like mysteries?"

"Yeah. When I have time to read, detective stories and thrillers are my jam."

"Huh, good to know."

I looked at the book and flipped it to read the reviews on the back. Then I opened the back cover. And saw a photo of the author, P. J. Monroe. I skimmed the description and regarded the photo again. My eyes see-sawed between it and Pete's face.

Oh, my goodness. I'd been harshly judging a famous author.

I leaned my forehead on my palm, shaking my head. I couldn't meet his gaze. Embarrassing didn't begin to describe the situation. Oh, good grief, I'm so stupid. All this time, too committed to the notion that I couldn't be interested in this man, I'd only searched for him online once.

"Hey, it's okay, Sylvie. I could've just told you what I did for a living, but you never asked. You're not knowing is entirely my fault."

Pete tapped my arm until I raised my head. He greeted me with the warmest smile. He wasn't angry at all.

"Please say something."

I grabbed my wine glass and tossed back the last bit. The acidity cut across my tongue as I swallowed.

"It's okay. I deserve this…this shaming."

"Shaming? What? No way. I've given no 'I'm a published author' vibe this past month. I'm renting that apartment because I had a flood after a pipe burst at my house."

I buried my head in my hands.

"Sylvie. It's okay."

"Were you laughing at me last night?"

"I was *not*. I deserved the judgment, so to speak. Keeping my life under wraps like that was wrong. I was certain you'd disappear after a quick while, so I didn't think you had to know anything about me."

I nodded, still a little speechless. I wasn't used to this version of Pete—talkative and vulnerable.

Remembering a book on his coffee table, I smiled. It had been a crime story written by a Richmond author. I had thought nothing of the signed page that read, "Pete, keep writing, Pat!"

"I bought you a gift. It's an apology, a 'let's reset our relationship' and Christmas gift all rolled into one."

"I have a gift for you, but I left it in Richmond, of course."

"Guess that means you have to come back."

"About that. My boss is adamant about me moving back here. I've got some stuff to work out."

"Obviously. We both have a lot to work out." He slid over a shimmery gold gift bag.

"Gorgeous bag. What is it?" I turned it around in a circle, holding it gingerly.

"Open it, silly woman."

White tissue landed all over the table before I pulled out a small box wrapped in gold paper and topped with a glittery gold bow. I shivered with excitement.

Inside the little box, I found a pair of white-gold snowflake earrings with tiny diamonds sparkling in the center. They were stunning and looked expensive. He watched me, and I wondered what he was thinking. A flush of warmth drifted down to my belly and up my neck—whole body involvement. Oh, the man made me crazy.

"I love snow!"

"I remember."

"Will you wait while I go to the ladies' room to put

them on?"

"I'm not going anywhere. We still have a dinner reservation to make. You better hurry."

When I returned, I held my hair up to show off my gift. I loved them and he knew it.

He stood up and placed his hands on my shoulders. "Ready for dinner?"

Our eyes met, and my heart skipped a beat.

I nodded and leaned in to kiss him on the cheek. His five-o'clock shadow offered a searing brush against my lips. I stepped back when I heard his intake of breath. We were seconds away from giving the pub customers a show, but I wanted our first kiss to be a little more spectacular.

Confession time: the kiss I expected from Pete would be the kind to make me tingle all over. A hot streak would run down the center of my body. I'd lift one foot off the ground and... I have seen an excessive number of romantic movies.

Our first kiss had occupied my brain since he took me to the Emergency Room. Not a romantic place at all, but what do they say about all great romances?

I dunno. I have no idea. But every woman gets what I mean, right?

As Pete helped me into my coat, I asked where we were dining.

"The concierge got us a table down the street. I know I promised we'd decide together, but Nashville is packed with visitors this week."

"Okay. I don't necessarily know everything I want in a man, but taking charge checks a box."

"Oy, the checklist, groan."

I laughed and swatted at him.

"Hey, I like this look." I gestured up and down in front of him. "Pretty hot, if you don't mind me saying."

"Thank you. Guess we're a handsome couple, yeah?"

I nodded, hoping my calm expression hid another rush of heat that flooded through me when he called us a couple. I wanted that and everything that went with it. I knew that included the good, the bad, and the ugly. My stomach clenched when I thought about fixing the mess with Pete and figuring out my work quandary.

The restaurant was busy and loud, but I got excited by the sight of white tablecloths and candles. Faint notes of a piano reached our corner table. Romantic.

Pete wasted no time asking his question when we returned our menus to the server, who was skinny and blonde and awfully pretty. I sighed inside, but Pete gave no impression that he'd noticed her beauty.

"How do I get you home to Richmond?"

I buttered a dinner roll. I didn't know how to answer him. I'd made no commitment to Patrick about moving to Nashville. I had a ticket to fly out the next day, Friday, which was also New Year's Eve. I kept my tone light.

"Flying is probably the best choice."

"Let's fly home together, then."

"I have a ticket—"

"I bought a one-way ticket, so I can work on a flight for us both."

"But—"

"No buts about it. I think we should fly home together. We have too much to talk about."

"Tomorrow's New Year's Eve."

While Pete chewed on his bread, he gestured with his knife like he was holding space for his words.

"Will you fly with me? I really am better at asking than demanding, I promise."

"Yes, I'll fly with you." I was eager to see how he pulled off the miracle of two seats on a holiday flight.

"What time can you finish work tomorrow?"

"I'd already planned to get to the airport by four for my flight. Is that okay? I can try to—"

"I'll work around your schedule. Prepare to be amazed."

He must have guessed I was doubting his abilities.

We clinked our glasses together.

"Whatever you say, PJ." I grinned at him across our plates, sizzling with steaks cooked rare.

"No, please, only Pete."

"Okay, 'only Pete.' "

"I have another question for you. It's more personal."

Oh no, I groaned inside. I gestured for him to go on, not trusting my voice.

"The online dating—"

"I deleted my account."

He frowned, making me wonder what concerned him still.

"When did you delete it? I'm just curious."

"You mean like when did I realize you could be 'the one'?" I patted his hand.

"I hadn't thought about it in that way. More like how many guys out there still have the number of this beautiful woman I want to keep in my life?"

"Pssshh…no worries there." I shook my head. "I'm totally available."

Pete lifted a glass. "To being totally available."

"Cheers." I clinked my glass against his, wishing I'd

said "I'm all yours" instead.

****

The next afternoon, when I texted him from my ride, Pete said to head to Gate Fifteen. The gate apparently had its own special entrance, and the driver had never taken that airport road. While I watched the fencing and planes slip by, he was fussing that we were going the wrong way.

And then we saw it. Me and James, the driver, both gasped. It was a private gate. I've never been near a private jet, but Pete stood at the base of a stairway leading up into a good-looking plane. It glistened white with gold and green lettering, like it was bound for Ireland or somewhere equally cool.

Pete met my driver at the car's trunk and retrieved my suitcase.

Out in that flat area, the wind flapped my coat. My hair blew all over my face and I wished I had a hat or scarf to tame it.

"This is our ride?" I gestured at the plane towering above us. To which Pete only smiled and rolled my case to the stairs, where a steward took possession of it.

"A friend helped me out."

"A friend?" I put it in air quotes. Pete shrugged.

I already liked his friend, and then I climbed the stairs and paused in the doorway. Whoa. Good golly, Miss Molly. Words of exclamation kept jumping around my brain. Oh, my goodness, I needed to send a selfie to Angie, but the timing wasn't right. I had to act like a grownup who'd been places north of Virginia, which I hadn't.

Pete guided me to a window seat. The cream-colored Italian leather felt like it was melting under my hands. I couldn't stop running my hands up and down both arms of the seat.

I murmured in awe, "Wow," and struggled to take in all the interior details. Pete just watched me with a whisper of a smile on his face.

A tall, black-haired man in a white shirt and navy pants stepped out of the cockpit.

"Sir, I need to file the flight plan."

"Give me a minute, Bob."

Pete squatted in front of me and took my hands in his.

"Sylvie. Um, tomorrow is Saturday. Do you have anywhere you have to be?"

I shook my head, raising my eyebrows in question. Weren't we bound for Richmond?

"There's a New Year's Day party. I want you to be my special date. The new year can be the fresh start we need."

"Where?"

"Just outside of New York City. At my publisher's place."

I sat back against the soft leather. What a surprising turn. Pete's expression never changed. Not a morsel of fear chased me. I was in it with Pete. He'd flipped my world upside down in the last month—his presence had mixed up my world. I can barely describe the horror his absence had brought. I'd missed him more than I'd cared to admit to myself or Angie.

"You can say 'no' and it'll be fine. I hadn't committed to attending because I flew out to Nashville."

"What's he like?"

"My publisher? Her name is Carol. She's a sweetheart and then a freaking Pitbull when she's mad."

"Hmm. I gotta meet her. Let's go." I was doing something spontaneous, something monumental even.

Pete stood and walked into the cockpit to deliver the news of our destination. He appeared to have done this a time or two. My stomach's resident butterflies fluttered with the reality of what I'd just agreed to. I sipped the champagne the steward had poured for us upon boarding. My skin fizzled with excitement, like the bubbles in my crystal flute.

The plane shuddered as the engines powered on. With a whistle of air and a soft thud, the steward closed the door we'd just come through.

Pete sat in the seat across the aisle from me and opened a black leather case. He pulled out a sheaf of paper.

"Is that—?"

"My latest novel?" Pete nodded.

"Can I read it? I mean, like, now?"

"You are its inspiration, so why not? But, fair warning. First drafts are notoriously…" He wiggled his hand.

When he began to hand it over, I waved him off. "Not exactly now. I need a minute to catch my breath."

"Me too, Sylvie, me too."

Ensconced in a private cocoon, I closed my eyes. I wanted to settle in, but I couldn't calm my fluttering heart. The year was ending, and my life might never be the same.

I glanced over at Pete, sitting rigid against his seat. With eyes closed, his dark lashes smudged his cheeks. I unbuckled my lap belt and got up quietly. A green blanket lay folded on the adjacent seat, so I fluffed it open and tucked it around him.

"Oh. Hey." He looked at me drowsily.

I sat beside him and slipped my hand in his.

"Hey."

"I thought you'd—"

I put a finger to his lips.

Pete and I studied each other, all wariness gone. The quiet roar of the jet engines filled the cabin.

"Up here, floating in the sky, you have to hear this. I started loving you the night you took me to the hospital. I'm sorry it took me so long to get here."

Pete kissed my knuckles. His gaze never flinched. He already felt my love.

"I beat you, but it isn't a contest."

I giggled and shook my head.

"No competing, except with ourselves. To love each other more each day?"

"Amen."

I kissed his fingertips, then smiled up at him.

"You said we'd fly home together because we have much to talk about. What's next on the topic list?

"I'll be headed to my house when we return to Richmond. My contractor texted me yesterday to say it's ready."

"Wow, that's awesome."

"I can't wait for you to see it."

"Do you have a fenced yard for Riley?"

"I sure do. He's gonna love it."

"Lots to smell? Like rabbits and deer?"

He barked out a laugh.

"What's so funny?"

"This. Not you, not at all. Just…I don't know. No New York City woman would ever ask about potential smells for doggie enjoyment."

I sat back, thinking. Pete was waiting for me to say something.

"And I reckon they wouldn't pick up after a dog either, would they?"

"Sylvie, Sylvie, you're a rare one. And no, they don't. Those city women pay people to do that."

"Geez Louise."

I closed my eyes. Pete's hand started slipping out of mine, and I squeezed it. I didn't want to lose contact.

"Hang on." I felt Pete moving around, and in seconds, he was covering me with his blanket. I cooed and snuggled under its warmth, keeping my eyes closed. When he returned to his seat, he pulled my head onto his shoulder.

"I'm sleepy, but I don't want to sleep with you finally beside me."

Pete took my hand and kissed it.

"I may never wash my hand again."

"Sleep, young lady."

I snuggled tighter against him and drifted off to a dream of Pete, me, and Riley in his back yard.

Chapter 28

Pete

Carol had hired a limo to collect us at the airport's private gateway. I thought Sylvie was going to faint over all the luxuries we were experiencing.

"What in the world?" she kept muttering over and over while her hand ran over the black-leather-clad space between us. When she caught my eye, she grinned like a crazy person.

"Are you used to this? Is this your life?"

I shook my head. I'm just an ordinary guy. Surely she'd believe that soon enough.

She peered out the window at the black sky cut into pieces by partially lit skyscrapers. A few buildings featured light designs for New Year's Eve. I didn't care about that and I doubted Sylvie did. It was getting late. Sleep was in our immediate future.

The shiny white limo whisked us to a midtown hotel, to separate rooms, of course. Sylvie started yawning as we neared the hotel. She needed to work on that, but I wasn't about to say a thing.

Carol's New Year's Day party started a little after noon. You never knew who you'd see each year. At this annual soiree, the guests drifted in and out over the course of the day, the party ending with fireworks at nine. Some years, I arrived early and missed the nighttime entertainment. It just depended on what was going on in my life.

On our first day in New York, I let Sylvie sleep undisturbed and didn't hear from her until almost two in the afternoon, which meant we were destined to hold some sparklers in the dark. I was looking forward to her seeing Carol's place. It was massive and tastefully decorated. I suspected Sylvie could hold her own with the crowd of New Yorkers she was about to meet. I just hoped she wouldn't bring up dog-walking.

While she slept, I bought myself a pair of dark wool slacks and a beige sweater for the party. I also started on book number twelve. My muse was back in my life—for good, I was certain. I had serious words flowing, and they needed to get out. It was a new year miracle, I suppose.

The biggest miracle was finding Sylvie ready to hear me out. And I had presented myself as ready to be open and authentic. Hard stuff for a wounded old guy.

We didn't arrive until the dinner buffet was set up. I surrendered my lovely date to the publishing mogul, Carol, who was overjoyed to see a woman on my arm.

After we both had created plates of tender beef and seared scallops, Sylvie eyed me at our small table. She had concerns about my career.

"So…" She leaned in with a pointed look. "You're still holding out on me. I cannot believe you."

Her eyes flashed. What had I done? Or not done, to be exact.

I leaned back with my hands raised in question.

"A movie deal? Really, Pete?"

"In my defense—"

Sylvie interrupted me with a raised hand. She did that a lot, didn't she?

"Remember that reset you offered when you gave me the earrings? These beautiful earrings."

"Yes," I offered tentatively.

"In the know. That's what I want between us. No secrets?"

"No secrets."

I wasn't sure how that would play out as we settled into this new relationship. But gosh, I loved the idea of being in a relationship. With Sylvie. Only her. She'd said, "us," hadn't she?

"How's your sister doing?"

Nice segue, right? I loved Sylvie's spark, but I wouldn't make it if she stayed irritated with me. I needed the love moments more than anything else.

"Sweet way to change the subject. Constance Miller is okay. She's still on bedrest. I've texted or called her nearly every day since. I sent her some magazines and a tea sampler. I'm just sorry I didn't get home for the holiday."

"Have you talked to Angie?"

"Uh-huh. You should read her hilarious texts. She's so happy. No, scratch that. You'd die if you saw how she blew up my phone."

I took her hand in mine, my thumb stroking her fingers. "Would you like to go to Alabama in a day or two? I might be able to make that happen."

Sylvie's eyes lit up, then clouded as the wheels started turning. She was so devoted to work; I suspected every thought spinning in her mind was trying to balance the work-versus-family issue. I let her finish her thinking process, which over the past few weeks I'd learned to appreciate.

Silence continued and I couldn't take it anymore.

"Can't you take any time off, Sylvie?" My gaze telegraphed my opinion of how her boss had taken advantage of her. She knew where I was coming from because we'd had a serious discussion about Patrick and her work during our dinner in Nashville.

"You'd take me to see my family?"

I nodded.

"Can I surprise 'em?"

I laughed out loud and grasped her hand again. "You bet."

She agreed to my suggestion that we linger in New York for another day or so to rest. She needed a break after everything she'd been through in the past few weeks. Two men—me and Patrick—had worn this beautiful woman out. But Sylvie had started a list of places to explore in the city, so maybe we'd stay longer before flying to Alabama. A surprise visit meant it didn't matter how long we stayed in the Big Apple.

I committed myself to helping her refresh so she could make the best decisions about her life. I had my own ideas about what her future might look like, but Sylvie had a mind of her own. An incredible, curious mind I deeply respected.

Sylvie made it to the fireworks part of the evening without yawning. She looked stunning in that green dress, and I'd caught other guests watching her. She'd added a curl to her dark blonde locks, even styling her hair so that her scars weren't fully covered. Quite a transformation, both physically and emotionally.

My brave and gorgeous muse was the total package.

I needed to stop calling her that, didn't I? She was way more to me than a vehicle for words. And the words I had were woefully inadequate to describe my heart's interior. Good thing I don't write romance books.

She stood in front of me on Carol's lawn. I slid my hand inside her coat and curved it around her waist, pulling her close. I liked her back pressed into me, like we were one. I rested my chin on the top of her head, which made her murmur and push tighter into me.

The sky sparkled red, gold, and purple. Pops and whistles filled the air over the river. We had a double show—in the sky and again as it reflected on the water.

"Are you real?" I whispered into Sylvie's ear.

She turned and looked up at me with a frown.

"What kind of question is that?"

"Questioning whether I have written some incredible new fiction. I mean, I'm not dreaming, right?"

"You are not dreaming. I'll show you."

She reached a hand behind my head, and I leaned in for her kiss. Do I have to tell you how many times I've imagined her lips on mine? Words again fail me.

"Come with me."

"Where are we going?"

She sounded perturbed that I'd interrupted her kissing mission. I was intent on kissing, too, but I had a different idea.

We walked up onto Carol's porch, holding hands. We could see the sky light up with fireworks and the murmurs of the awed guests, but we were alone. I pulled her behind a potted tree.

"Now, what were you going to show me, Ms. Bradley?"

Low laughter bubbled out of her, making me want to hold her even more.

"Oh, you."

I saw her lips curve into a smile through the

darkness, brimming with possibilities. Those lips called to me, and I could wait no longer. My fingers brushed her cheek before they dug into her hair. I pulled her against me, knees to heads our bodies touching.

"Sylvie."

She wrapped her arms around my neck, offering herself. I took her mouth in mine. Our lips searched and tasted each other. This woman had shocked my heart with feelings I thought I'd never experience again. My brain crackled with the newness of Sylvie, so soft and pure.

I kissed my way down to her neck. Her delicate perfume enchanted all my senses as I nibbled her ear. Sylvie's fingers knotted in my hair as she gasped. I moaned softly against her cheek. We were making enough noise together to tune out the clamor of fireworks.

I let my lips drift over her forehead. She jerked back and studied me through moody gray eyes. My fingers gently glided over the shiny skin, the ridges and valleys unyielding to my touch. Sylvie closed her eyes, permission for me to kiss her scars again. Caressing what she hated about herself was my token of deepest love. A sigh of surrender escaped her.

I pulled away and looked into her eyes. Her face was flushed, and her eyes now sparkled—with happiness or tears, I couldn't be sure. Perhaps both. I brushed a thumb across her bottom lip, eliciting a quiet whimper from my beautiful muse.

One hand rested on my chest, the heat of it chasing away the chill of the dark night. I wrapped my hand around it and kissed the tips of her fingers, never taking my eyes off hers. Sylvie's lips parted, pleasure lighting up her face.

"I'm going to love you forever, Sylvie."

"Forever's a long time."

"And long enough to fill a library, my darling muse."

She giggled at my joke, so I kissed her lips again.

The fireworks sizzled and popped in the sky above us, and we made our own on the edge of Carol's frosted lawn.

It promised to be a year for the books.

A word about the author...

Julie is a teacher at heart. She spent most of her career in higher education. But all the while, she read lots of books and dreamed.

She lives in Virginia with her dogs and near her three adult children.

juliejranson.com

Thank you for purchasing
this publication of The Wild Rose Press, Inc.

For questions or more information
contact us at
info@thewildrosepress.com.

The Wild Rose Press, Inc.

www.ingramcontent.com/pod-product-compliance
Ingram Content Group UK Ltd.
Pitfield, Milton Keynes, MK11 3LW, UK
UKHW020658151224
452011UK00009B/40

9 781509 258390